On the Great-

Simon and Schuster / New York

Circle
Route
a novel by
Lucienne S. Bloch

Copyright © 1979 by Lucienne S. Bloch
All rights reserved
including the right of reproduction
in whole or in part in any form
Published by Simon and Schuster
A Division of Gulf & Western Corporation
Simon & Schuster Building
Rockefeller Center
1230 Avenue of the Americas
New York, New York 10020

Designed by Irving Perkins
Manufactured in the United States of America
1 2 3 4 5 6 7 8 9 10

Library of Congress Cataloging in Publication Data

Bloch, Lucienne S
    On the great-circle route.

    I. Title.
PZ4.B65240n [PS3552.L553] 813'.5'4 79-13874
ISBN 0-671-24817-0

This book is for my mother,
my father, and for C.

Part One

Pas Devant les Enfants

I

I came with my parents to live on the Upper West Side of New York. We came first-class on what they tell me was the maiden voyage of the *Nieuw Amsterdam,* my parents dancing their way to a new world through the famous hurricane in September of 1938. I have a photograph of them sitting at the Captain's Table. My mother is bare-armed, clearly pregnant, flirtatious, her glass half-raised to salute the occasion. My father bristles, his hair so short, so black; in his large dark eyes you can see the sharpness that made him take seriously every word of *Mein Kampf* when he first read it and recognized Hitler's scheme as one of the more calamitous probabilities of modern politics. In the photograph, Thomas Mann, looking tired, sits at the table with them. I was an infant, traveling with a nurse. I must have cried when those winds blew.

My parents had at first no intention of altering their life and thought to suit America. They had both lived, as children and growing up, in many different countries and it was evident to them that regional arrangements, nationality and so on, were hardly useful. Like other wealthy refugees from Hitler's Europe who arrived here early and in their habitual high style, not fleeing, exactly, my parents kept their local adjustments to a bare and obstinate minimum. Some animals, giraffes, say, or bobwhites in dry grass, fawns and flounder, finding themselves in a strange or possibly threatening situation, will make use of at least a thin veneer of any protective coloration that may be available to them. With a bit of luck, they blend into the landscape and dappled safety. My parents felt no need, and certainly no inclination, for the cosmetic aspects of assimilation. Such camouflage was not just banal, it was unhistorical, unnecessary. Because they were educated and had money and rules and a good business in their pockets, and because the war that was still developing would have to be over pretty soon, my parents considered themselves transients here, as elsewhere. They were formed, self-sufficient, quite all right the way they were, thanks.

I do not know if on their own my mother and my father would have been able to maintain such an overtly alien posture for as long as they did. But my parents emigrated from Antwerp in a large and luxurious wave that was made up of my father's outsized family and an entire crowd of friends who agreed: there would be no melting, none at all, in this particular pot. They quickly threw up walls around their world to keep the natives out, much as did the earliest settlers in respect to the savages they encountered on this continent. Some of those walls still stand, such foolish fences. I didn't speak a lot of English when I went off to school, in spite of having lived six years in New York with parents who had both spoken that language eloquently since their own school days. It took that many years, three American-born children, and a Europe smashed by war and genocide, unforeseen and unendurable, to produce in my parents even a small linguistic concession to the fact that their life was and would continue to be in America.

When my sisters were born, four years after my brother to the very day, there were more than perceptible shifts in our household. We had already moved to a larger apartment in the same building. But premature twins were more than any ordinary nurse would take on alone, so my mother called back into her home the Belgian girl who had come with us to America as my nursemaid. This capable person had, in the interim, produced a child of her own without bothering to marry. He came too. There were five young children, two baby nurses, a governess for my brother and me, a cook, a chambermaid-waitress, a laundress and, occasionally, a seamstress. Everyone lived in but the governess and the laundress and, it seemed, my parents, who quite understandably went out day and night.

My brother and I and the nurse's boy would be having our supper, all milky soft food, when my parents would look in to say goodnight. We never minded their leaving because once they were gone we could get on to the main event of the day: dropping cottage cheese bombs twelve stories down onto Central Park West. We sometimes varied our attack with ink or spit but nothing else ever had the resonance, the plop, of cottage cheese. A doorman would rush upstairs, the two nurses denied responsibility; the governess, who had escaped soon after serving our supper, could not be found; we blamed the nurse's boy. We were unstoppable, my brother and I. Goldfish died belly-up in bright red water, scissors were found in the babies' cribs, there was chewing gum (stolen from the cook) under the piano keys, Chinese figurines were dramatically decapitated, the cod-liver oil disappeared regularly, and our governess-knit woolen underpants were unraveled stitch by stitch as fast as that misguided woman could come up with new ones. We kept on blaming the nurse's boy, who developed some rather ugly mannerisms as a defense against our overwhelming meanness.

Life was difficult if not intolerable in our house and

some changes had to be made. The nurses left, one with her blameless twitching boy, and were replaced by a Scottish shrew whose good friend, equally severe, came in to take care of the babies on Nanny's day off. Our governess, the daughter of a friend of a friend, was fired and rehired at least twelve times in as many months. She finally left, permanently confused and disheartened, I fear. My parents stayed home more often and my brother and I had to eat with them in the dining room when they didn't have company. There were always five or six pieces of heavy silver flatware laid around each plate and we were taught to use all that cutlery with a nimble and indifferent precision. My parents mentioned school frequently but unspecifically. We were to get allowances, in return for which we had to be nice, nicer, to each other and the help. We agreed to that.

My father had a big gray LaSalle, an automobile to match his mood and girth. Every June in those early years he would drive us to Lake Placid, where we spent the summer. Lake Placid was chosen because of its resemblance to Switzerland, its good air, and a large hotel called the Grandview, which was filled with other Europeans who also saw the Swiss likeness and loved *luft*. We, too numerous and noisy for hotel life, took houses, often the same one on Fawn Hill. My father, having delivered us, did a vanishing act. Was he in Hong Kong, or Johannesburg, or just at home in the cool of solitude? My father must have flown up for a few guest appearances on weekends, but I don't remember seeing him much in the summertime.

In her attempt at rustic simplicity—somewhat in the manner of Marie Antoinette—and perhaps in order not to alarm our neighbors on Fawn Hill, who were in fact simple people, my mother cut back on her domestic arrangements in the summer. She never took a governess or a cook to Lake Placid, and the Belgian nurse and her boy went elsewhere in the summers of the years they lived in our house. My mother managed with just a nurse for the twins, who were more than less caged in their playpens under a huge maple tree in our garden. Two locals, sisters, came in daily to deal with our various mess. We took many of our evening meals, my mother, my brother and I, at a boardinghouse on Hillcrest Avenue that was run by a spinster with an undeniable passion for paper doilies whose edges, limp and stained, curled over many of the plates on her tables. Miss O'Connor served us soup as tepid as her smile and meat that wasn't much friendlier. It was an establishment that turned me off restaurants at a very early age. In the mornings, my mother took us to a private beach on Mirror Lake for our swimming lessons. She spent her afternoons at the Grandview, on the tennis courts or out of sight and, in the summer that I remember best, left my brother and me on our own after lunch.

Miraculously free from supervision, my brother and I would walk down into the town after our required hour of rest. Large chunks of our afternoons were passed watching people go in and out of the movie house on Main Street. By the end of July we were ready and, shaking, went in one day with the rest of the crowd. We had to sit in the children's section, up front, under the surveillance of a matron in a white uniform. We had not anticipated the existence of such a person, whose roving flashlight picked out and froze the faces of overloud bubble gum poppers and those rowdies who had their feet on the seat in front of them. The first movie we happened to see was *Lifeboat*. Even with the little English I had I could make out most of the story. Cannibalism, amputations, group murder, and the burning sun that destroyed minds; I drank in the juice of indiscriminate disaster. We had been taken to the movies before, in New York, to see suitable Disneys, but Tallulah Bankhead was a far cry from Bambi. My brother and I immediately agreed to cut out of our lives all expenses related to candy and comic books and we saved our allowances so that we could go back often for more of the same. One day, exiting at four-thirty from a fierce Cagney film, we bumped right into my mother, who was looking at the billboards. At first she didn't seem to recognize us. Then, quickly enough, what was happening dawned on her and she grabbed one of my braids and my brother's arm and pulled us both uphill and home. Once there, she took her stiff Kent hairbrush and applied it with great vigor to the appropriate places. From that afternoon on and for a couple of summers thereafter, a baby-sitter came every day after lunch to take us on educational walks in the pinewoods. We collected so many wild flowers, butterflies and well-shaped, well-streaked rocks that the attic of the house on Fawn Hill came to look like a storage room for nature's surplus because we were never allowed to take our collections back to the city.

After we got back from Lake Placid that summer, my brother and I started school. My parents, finally convinced that we were here to stay, could no longer postpone our formal education. We were enrolled in school, lessons were arranged, obligations and expectations delineated neatly and with a kind of humorous intensity that I never found too funny. Having settled us, my mother turned with missionary energy to her special task, the civilizing of this large and needy country. It would take time, but she was strong and willing. I believe she intended to do this by setting up models of such splendid culture and refinement (her children) that imitators (her soon-to-be American friends and their children) would flock and flourish under her Mitteleuropean aegis. To make models, two things were necessary: rules and lessons. We certainly had our fill of both.

The rules were easy to learn, less easy to interpret. For example, on Mondays we had lamb chops. Having lamb chops on Mondays had something to do with the icebox being cleaned after the weekend, according to a list of routine duties posted for the cook on the inside of the door of the broom closet in the kitchen. It takes me back, those lamb chops on schedule: grease on my mouth, the butcher's frill, a handle. Rules were rules. Whether it was lamb chops or piano-practicing rules or company rules or religious rules or hair and dress rules didn't matter very much. What mattered was that our lives at home were governed by rules from day to day, from then to now. I suppose you could say it was practical, in a large family, to lay down rules like tracks we could ride on. No bumping, no passing, no straggling. But those rules had a sharp reality beyond the merely efficient or decorative. They seemed to me to be totems loaded with powerful tribal spirit. If obeyed, they would insure protection and success. If broken or debased in any way, failure. It sounds ridiculous but it worked. Rule-making-and-testing time was dinner. The dining room became a battlefield, growing bloodier with each year that passed. Big and smaller guns roared in the home-front skirmishes of wills and wants just as they roared in the Europe my parents had left in body if not exactly, entirely, in spirit. As oldest, I scouted for the rest of the children. What I had to do was to map a new continent.

I don't dream much, or not recollectably so. I rise mornings with no sense of anything missing, anything puzzling. I have a lot of white nights but they are dreamless. I suppose that dreams are useful diagrams, figures in a carpet we all walk on, and I suppose that we rise each day to flesh out those figures with the weight of our very own bones and breath. Without a diagram it takes a little longer, moves less clearly. I do have one dream and I have it because I remember dreaming it so many times as a child. In Pilgrim dress, white-collared-and-capped, I lead an excited crowd up Riverside Drive toward the George Washington Bridge. We all run and yell and the men wave sticks so it seems we are attacking but I feel we are fleeing. On our left, the river chops and snorts spray in plumes that catch and mangle the sunlight. The big bridge glints against a so-blue sky and there is a traffic jam on its span that I fear will block us Pilgrims. That's about it, a running dream. Perhaps it came from a Thanksgiving play we did in school one year and maybe it didn't. Plays were such a large part of our scholastic life that they could have been important to me, but I can't recall the event as I can the dream.

Under ordinary circumstances, school eats up children and their time in it. Big gulps of the day, long years, disappear down academic craws and are eventually regurgitated in the guise of information and a method or two. The school I went to did nothing like that. We got a minimum of information, developed few marketable skills, and time was something we had plenty of on our hands. My brother and I were sent to a "progressive" school. More out of convenience than conviction, I believed. It was across the street from where we lived. Never mind about the omnipotence of rules at home and the lack of any rules at all in school: that kind of inconsistency could be and was overlooked with an ease that astonishes.

Everything in those first six years in The Walden School was done in circles. In circle time we heard stories, had juice, and sat at little round tables to practice little round numbers. We took our rests in circles, on blue canvas cots with our feet pointed inward so that whatever germs we might be harboring would not spread too fast. Most often, we voted in circles. We had to vote on absolutely everything. We voted on whether to do blocks or painting, on whether to have saltines or graham crackers for snack, on going to roof or park and, very soon, on whether to study China or Washington, D.C. The group was the main thing and the group decided. Even after I was fluent in English I had trouble taking it all in. What baffling possibility! Each vote was preceded by a great deal of discussion which got, as I guess it was meant to, very political. Early on in first grade, power blocs formed that swung votes and curricula for the rest of us for years to come. We called our teachers by their first names and were on such intimate terms with them that we often hit them as we did each other. One day in circle, in my second year, a boy threw his little chair at the teacher's head and laid her out flat on the floor. He was moved one class higher the next day. Was that a punishment? I wasn't sure. We spent a lot of time in shop or in the nature room, waiting for a turn at the lathe or with the rabbits. We made innumerable salad bowls and bookends but nobody ever voted for geography.

This kind of schooling left me with more than enough time and energy to concentrate on my real education, my after-school. I took piano, ballet, French, speech, riding, Hebrew and went to Saturday Group and Sunday School. Seasonally, tennis and skating were added. In some years much of this took place in one week and some lessons I had twice a week. Like a chicken ready to be roasted, I was trussed and larded with fragrant disciplines. On long thin legs, balancing traditional Jewish ambitions, I scrambled around New York in an educational frenzy. From school, about which I remember very little, I rushed to after-school, about which I remember everything. My mother, the proud recipient of a similarly promiscuous education in Vienna, didn't believe in free time or school friends. When I had a minute, we dropped into a museum. When I had five minutes, we went to see my grandparents, either set would do.

Huge gatherings of my father's family took place, molelike, at night and with a dismal frequency. Every Friday night after dinner, to be precise. On that side I had ten aunts and uncles and thirteen cousins close in age and more often than not we were all there at once. There was lemon tea in a glass, cookies from Holland with slivers of almonds on them, and Oriental rugs to focus on when the conversation was in a language we couldn't follow. Besides French, which we spoke, most of us had listening capabilities in German and Dutch. Polish and Malay were spoken when adult privacy was imperative. You can see that the diamond business produced its share of polyglots. My grandfather sat in his chair by the window, high above West End Avenue, feudally scattering blessings and the promise of silver dollars, payable when the Sabbath had ended, to those children who truly deserved them. The long living room had beige walls and blue velvet chairs and, in one corner near the hall, a right-angled arrangement of blue velvet couches. The grown-ups sat on chairs near my grandfather. All of the children sat, literally cornered, on those couches, knees touching. We were summoned one at a time to my grandfather to report on the week's achievements. There were no failures. We didn't really report to my grandfather directly because none of us could speak his languages. He had somehow bypassed French. Our parents spoke for and about us, with additional commentary provided by whichever aunt or uncle happened to be on the spot. If we had learned a new prayer in Hebrew School that week, we were asked to recite it. Those were the weeks I didn't get a dollar, on purpose.

My father's father was an old man all of his life, my mother says. By the time I knew him there was little left but a husk, bleached-out and dry. My grandmother was as robust as he was frail, but no younger, no softer. Together they had left Poland-when-it-was-Austria, had borne and raised six children in Holland, and moved from there to Belgium and finally to New York. Along the way they had increased considerably a family fortune. Mainly by not spending it. Extremely pious, they also demanded from their children total obedience to the laws of Jewish family life. This, they must have reckoned, would keep their clan intact. They were right for almost a whole generation. In this family's gyrations from country to country, from continent to continent, they were like the Great Wallendas: self-supportive, accomplished, elegant, close. There were only three truants in that tribe. My father and his outlandish Viennese wife, my mother, were two of them. I always knew that my father's position was more of a force-out by his siblings than intentional on his part. The third renegade was an unobtrusive man married to my father's older sister, and he seemed as out of place in that family as I wanted and felt myself to be. He was a furrier among diamond people, a reader among gossipers, a German among Poles with pretensions, partially deaf, a misfit. I liked my uncle because he paid some uncritical attention to me. Simple. My uncle was so mild and dear a man that his truancy was as negligible in family eyes as my parents' was not.

My father's brothers and sisters were, all of them, as pious as their parents. Except for my father and his older sister, they had all married young men and women from Antwerp whose parents were also in the diamond business and whose piety matched their own. They all worked together, prayed together, went on vacation together, and sent their children to the same parochial school and summer camp. We, my mother and her brood, were the foreigners. Not only was my mother a bankrupt banker's daughter, but she had rejected her parents' orthodoxy early in her adolescence. It wasn't, after all, the sort of thing you hung on to in post-Freudian Vienna. She did not conceal this defection from her peers, my aunts and uncles, probably figuring that they would understand and accept what their parents would not. They didn't. And to add yet another layer to our alien cake, my mother was beginning, definitely, to send out daring feelers of friendship toward the young mothers whom she met at our school. She had insisted that we go to a real American school and that we start with all those expensive lessons. She won that round. Some rounds that she lost got us sent to a Jewish camp one summer, to The Jewish Center in winter, and into a more or less permanent state of siege. Were we the prizes for the winners of these fights? I didn't feel like a prize. I felt more like the canvas on the floor of a ring in which two pros exercised their considerable skills. My father, with some fancy footwork, tried hard to hide from his parents the extent of what they would consider our heretical assimilation. He was an overly attentive son, hoping that way to stuff up the cracks that were spreading so rapidly between them and us, between himself and his brothers and sisters. I do not believe that anyone was fooled.

When we went to visit my mother's parents we got no dollars because they really had none to spare. My grandfather, a formerly high-living private banker, had made and lost fortunes as often as other people dusted their books. I am told that he wrote poetry in his youth, kept horses and women, took his own kosher chef to the French Riviera, where he spent part of every winter at the Négresco in Nice, all of this in better days. My mother's family too had moved from Poland to Holland and had settled, between wars, in Vienna. There were four children, all beautiful, then and still difficult. My grandfather considered himself such an important person in Vienna's financial life that he was sure his being Jewish would be overlooked by the authorities, Nazi and other. What arrogance! Of course he was wrong and trapped, separated from my grandmother, who was making her way alone to London, via Dunkerque as it turned out, where her other daughter lived. My grandfather and his two sons, whom he had insisted on keeping by his side, finally managed to buy their way out of a French internment camp near Marseille and they arrived in New York late in 1941, my grandfather having lost everything but that treacherous arrogance of his. My grandmother came soon after the war ended and my father set them up in a small hotel apartment close to where we lived. There were no cousins here, no velvet couches, no tests, only those two people whose German didn't sound right to us. My grandmother kept honey drops for us in a bowl that had red birds painted around its rim. She had a pile of our picture books and was trying to teach herself English. I would read aloud with her, and tell her the names of things while pointing to them, but we couldn't really talk except to say "gin rummy" to each other. My grandfather was forever on the telephone, trying to put back together the shards of a life.

For the sake of my mother's parents, we belonged to a little *shul* next door to their hotel. They couldn't afford and wouldn't accept seats in the synagogue my father's family attended. Not wanting them to worship alone, my mother got my father to agree to join this tiny congregation, housed on the ground floor of a brownstone that was derelict long before anyone knew what urban blight was. How she won that particular round I'll never know. The sermons were delivered in Yiddish, the air was foul, and we were the star ornaments in that small room. Naturally, we had to dress the part. In those days wool was wool, September meant new clothes and the High Holy Days, and the hottest day of the year was always Yom Kippur, when you had to wear those new woolen clothes on an empty stomach. We'd start off to *shul* in the morning like horses on parade before the big race. Outfits, that's what we wore, with gloves and hats and cast-iron shoes. The Emperor's offspring in their brand-new clothes marched down 86th Street, nodding to friends in the crowd, smiling queerly, wishing we too could enter those luminous synagogues filled with people we knew who spoke our language. When no one was looking, we ducked quickly around a corner and up another street and into that dark house we were ashamed to acknowledge as a temple.

My father, the big contributor, had a seat of honor near the Rabbi's pulpit. My mother, the big contributor's wife, sat next to the Rabbi's wife in the front row of a section in the back of the room that was just curtained off from the main space. In real synagogues, we knew, the women got to sit upstairs and could see and be seen. My brother, not yet a Jewish man, could sit wherever he chose to. He often chose the steps outside. We three woolly daughters, itching terribly, sat as far back as was possible and muttered. I know, I know, I set a very bad example. We had stashed comic books under the jackets of our suits and we folded them carefully into the prayer books for a good read. We jingled our charm bracelets, we squeaked our shoes, we coughed and giggled, we sang dirty songs under our breath, anything, to help us pretend that we were not there and not a part of those people around us. Finally, my mother would turn and glare wildly in our direction. We took this as permission to join my brother outside. We wouldn't talk to any of those other children. The boys had long curls twisted around their ears. They all spoke Yiddish to each other. Their families had never made it to Belgium or Vienna. They smelled. They could tell we weren't religious like them.

We could have prayed along with the best of them if we had wanted to. All four of us in our middle years spent no less than two, sometimes three, afternoons a week in Hebrew School. When it came to our education nothing was too good, so we didn't have to study Hebrew in that little *shul*. We went instead to a palace of orthodoxy approved by my father's family, *The* Jewish Center. It had marble walls, large bright classrooms equipped with pull-down maps and blackboards, not one but two elevators, and a stage with a complex lighting system designed to clarify the plays that the older classes put on for what was supposed to be our entertainment and edification. The J.C. looked good, it smelled fine, they even had brownies for snack. But we were as estranged in that palazzo as we were in the tenement, in spite of having a few school friends and some cousins in our classes. For one thing, we never showed up for Services. Where did we go? was a question we never wanted to answer. For another thing, everyone knew, here too, that we, that my mother wasn't really religious. My cousins told them that we were fakes. We were discovered.

Even the teachers knew and old Mr. Marcus, waxy and foxy, seemed to delight in using that knowledge against us. Being so close in age, my brother and I were often put in the same grade in Hebrew School. My brother would raise his hand, wanting to leave the room for a quite standard purpose. Mr. Marcus would ask him, every time, if he was wearing the proper ritual fringes under his shirt. He never asked anyone else. My brother is not a liar and of course he always said no, which meant he couldn't leave the room. I know he sometimes had to pee discreetly down the leg of his pants. I know because I sat next to him when I could, thinking to protect him, to distract Marcus or at the very least to put an extra body between the mess he made and the rest of the class. This went on for some time until, miraculously, my brother was able to control his bladder in those difficult circumstances. Later, when my brother began to prepare his Bar Mitzvah, my father hired Mr. Marcus to coach him. Twice a week for many months Mr. Marcus would ring our doorbell, just after dinner, and come into our house. I couldn't believe it!

My brother is a performer. He always got the lead in school plays. He was a cherubic blond fatty who took center stage every time he opened his mouth, anywhere. Jokes tumbled casually from his lips, he could play jazz piano, he was popular, he listened, he never got a good grade in his life. I, older by less than a year, was sharp and shy, quick to cry, with a very nasty temper. Together we might have made up one whole person. The finest performance I ever saw my brother give was in camp the first summer we were sent away from home. We went, along with that multitude of tattling cousins, to a camp in the Adirondacks that promised anxious parents the *strictest* observance of Jewish dietary and Sabbatical obligations. They were pretty lax about everything else at Camp North Star. We didn't have to swim, canoe, play baseball, practice knots or at any time clean our bunks if we didn't want to. Tennis and hospital corners were unknowns. That was the summer I learned to play a vicious game of jacks. What we did have to do at Camp North Star was appear every morning at assembly, write home

twice a week, and wear dress uniforms on Friday nights
and all day Saturday, when we had to go to Services in
the Rec Hall. Wooden benches were laid out in rows
across the room, with counselors stationed on the ends of
every bench to enforce quiet.

One day early in August a holiday new to my brother
and me was mentioned. A day of fasting, *Tishah b'Ov.*
For a week before this fast day three of my female cousins saw it as their duty to inform the rest of the camp
that, of course, my brother and I would not be fasting.
We were scarcely Jews, they said, scarcely fit to talk to.
Not daring to face that day, my brother and I got up early
and walked deep into the woods instead of going to assembly. We spent the long day gorging on just-ripe blue-
berries, swatting mosquitoes, telling knock-knock jokes.
It was one of our best times together. No one came to
look for us because they were all too busy praying. We
came back to camp late at night, our dress whites
streaked purple, and sneaked into our bunks. The next
morning while announcements were being made around
the flagpole our names were called. We both stepped forward, out of the ranks once again. I immediately stumbled into tears and thereby avoided questioning. My
brother listened serenely to the accusations and threats
and when asked by the head counselor, Uncle Morty, to
answer for himself raised his right arm high and said,
"Heil Hitler!" What timing! What presence! The whole
camp cracked up. I howled. My mother arrived that
afternoon to take us away.

That summer set just a few things straight. My brother
and I were, whenever possible, to be separated. We
would no longer share a room or our summers. We were
trouble, again. Beds were shuffled around and my sisters, then about six, moved into my room and my life. I
zoned them neatly into one end of that large room. There
was a deep and dangerous river full of famished croco-
diles that ran, I said, between us. They believed me and

in my power in a way my brother never would. The bathroom, being on my side, presented a small problem. Luckily for them I was away all day at school and every afternoon was occupied. I was by then in the full throes of all those lessons, trying at once to absorb and relate that crush of information and technique. Always in a hurry, I was being imprinted for life and for marriage. It was a rush job.

The one slow part of my week was spent in a dim corridor waiting my turn for the piano teacher. I took lessons for eight years from a White Russian Princess who lived in what I believed was a truly romantic state of exile on 88th Street. I would arrive as early as I could, clutching a scrappy Schirmer's envelope, and sit in the narrow hall hoping to catch a glimpse of the Princess's son on his way to the kitchen. A spidery boy, but older, intriguing in the half-light. Soon the hysterical Czerny exercises on the other side of the door would stop. It was my turn. A curtsy to the Princess. I played badly, too methodically, too loudly, and as hard as I tried I knew my music would never lure that noble boy out of the kitchen and into my arms. The Princess was tall, hissed, and believed in metronomes. She balanced books on my head to keep me sitting up straight at the keyboard. I was never able to memorize music and had to depend on reading the notes, fast. Every time I leaned toward the music rack, when the page was at its blackest, the books would fall on my hands and the lesson would be over. I couldn't be dismissed until my time was actually up, so I would sit in a corner while the Princess played Chopin or Scarlatti as she thought such music should be played. I would look at old photographs in green leather albums of the Princess and her family in their royal period. The history was better than the music. Once a year the Princess hired Steinway Hall and presented her pupils with their varying proficiencies to an audience that forgave us everything. My performances were shameful, my eyes squeezed shut to goad my memory and contain the tears that, if they fell on my fingers, wouldn't help matters at all. The Princess sat on the aisle in the front row, wearing a long velvet dress, her large head nodding, nodding, brisker than any mere mechanical device.

Every Thursday afternoon after school for two years that I remember too well, my brother and I would get on the number ten bus for our weekly journey into Hell. White House, Beresford, Kenilworth, Dakota, Majestic, Century. The names of the buildings on Central Park West tolled us downtown and into the Devil's waiting room. My brother and I lisped. Correction was mandatory. We spent an hour a week with Dr. Froeschmann, who worked on us like Pavlov sweating over his dogs. We had to hold electrodes to both sides of our throats while we read aloud passages from Sherlock Holmes and the major American humorists. Our choice. One overly sibilant *sssss* and the juice went up, O save me! Everything buzzed and we gagged and sobbed and Froeschmann roared with laughter at those paragraphs we choked on, O save me now! Froeschmann, frog-faced as named, was a fiend if ever I met one. He spoke a brand of English that bore absolutely no resemblance to that perfection in whose name we were electrocuted once a week. Round, rimless Froeschmann, oozing Froeschmann, bastard, you bastard. Of course it never worked. I lisp now, my children lisp, my children's children will lisp in triumph over the forces of remembered evil. And what a trap those hours were. If we so much as considered self-pity, we were demolished. Tears were just an involuntary reflex and so, probably, could be discounted. No matter how determined we were on any one Thursday to stay calm and articulate, that demon just turned up the current and undid our best resolves. The way to handle the situation was, as in camp, to disappear. We got lost as often as we dared. We'd get on the subway, rationalizing that we were late, and fetch up happily in Brooklyn or Queens two hours later. I, oldest and responsible, would call home to explain our predicament. The police would arrive a few minutes later to escort us home. Beatings followed dinner on those days but no one ever thought to cancel Dr. Froeschmann.

I liked my sporting lessons best, the riding and ballet and skating, even though I never won a ribbon or made it onto those precious toe shoes. I liked the actual exertions and I liked even more the fact that they were not private lessons. In these classes I took there were girls from other worlds across the Park where you went to school each day dressed in navy blue or plaid tunics that had to cover your knees completely. In the various changing rooms we shared, these girls slipped out of their clothes so quickly, so unashamedly, their bare skin gleaming pink like icing on some white cupcakes. I always wondered if wearing uniforms made what was underneath seem uniform too, a regulation and acceptable body. Listening in, I overheard words that confounded me. For years I thought that prep periods were some premenstrual condition I was missing out on. Field days and drilling with the grays, something brothers did, I knew, but what exactly? These girls danced and filled up cards at junior assemblies; in assembly we saw movies or heard the lower-school orchestra play the "Toy Symphony" for perhaps the fiftieth time. It couldn't be the same thing at all. Changed, we'd trot in the ring or do figure eights or *grands battements* for an hour and I looked just like the rest of them.

Unlike my teachers at school, whose severities were more laughable than not, the teachers I had for afterschool seemed to be as strict as it was possible to be within the confines of a simply human relationship. Madame Allard, who for many years led me through the tenuous reaches of post-Diderotic French, had a nose as thin and sharp as the remarks she made about my tin ear and my miserable handwriting. She wore a gray suit, summer and winter, with a little lace-edged handkerchief tucked triangularly into her breast pocket. Peeping from the folds of that flag was a tiny bunch of mauve felt violets. I knew that in France the language of flowers is a very precise one but I could never figure out those violets. They certainly didn't stand for tenderness. Madame Allard's passion, if one existed, was for the poetry of Victor Hugo and Lamartine. When I was older, as a sop to what she considered my untidy and adolescent sensibilities, we sometimes read aloud from the work of Verlaine. Tears rolled down my cheeks as they rained from the sky, dripping on my *dictée* and earning me a bad mark for the day. I was longing for Paris, for poets, for sonorous speech that always seemed to mean so much more than it said, and what I got was Madame Allard's discourse number forty-five on the uses of the pluperfect subjunctive with a little aside on the well-documented dangers of drinking the water. The topography of France was another of Madame Allard's reluctant passions and we spent many hours drilling the names of rivers, mountain ranges and *départements*. Give me a blue pencil and I can still draw the course of the Loire and its tributaries.

There were afternoons when I came home late, after lessons, to hear ancient lamentations in our living room. Another relative on my mother's side, sometimes a distant one, sometimes closer, would have surfaced in New York. These people had numbers tattooed on their arms and horror etched forever in their eyes. I would be introduced and told to sit down, too old by now to be exempted from atrocity. I didn't need to know the language they spoke because what they said was clear enough and what they didn't say was clearer still. I, Frenchy and fancy, squirmed, pleaded homework, wanting out. There was a girl who came one day with her mother, a girl exactly my age. She had been hidden for eight years by a Polish farmer and was now a devout and lumpy Catholic, a peasant who didn't call her mother "mother" because as far as she knew that lady wasn't her real one. I had to give that girl half of everything I had: clothes, jewelry, even half my bed for the week it took her parents to find an apartment. I was ungracious in the giving and slapped for it in front of her. When my father came home on those afternoons he would immediately get on the telephone and start arranging jobs and housing and contacts. His wallet would fly open, my mother would offer, and there was more wailing about the shame of it. I was impressed by the amounts he gave, wondering if there would be enough left for us and of course there was, there always was enough.

II

The Ostend Hotel on the boardwalk in Atlantic City was a hotel that catered, kosherly, to Jews of the Diaspora who when they saw the sea didn't always know what to make of it. We are not a very pelagic people. Once a year for several years when I was ten and eleven and thereabouts, I went to the Ostend with my father's older sister, an aunt who thought she was doing me a big favor by taking me along with her own two girls, with whom I shared a room that was not meant for three. Or was the favor to my mother, who welcomed a midseason vacation from me? My father's entire family, us excepted as usual, traveled to Atlantic City for Passover every year. They were people who really cared about things like changing the dishes and burning the bread, but were just the tiniest bit lazy when it came to doing or even supervising those chores. So, once again, exodus made sense. My favorite aunt on my father's side, married to one of my father's brothers and therefore not a real aunt, was emancipated enough to insist on staying at the Ritz, farther down the boardwalk, although she took her main meals at the Ostend. As she had two boys, I was not asked to stay at the Ritz, where I felt I belonged, with them.

During a Seder, the Passover feast, you get to dip your fingers in a full wineglass ten times, once for each of the ten plagues visited by God upon the Egyptians to induce them, somewhat sadistically I thought, to let the Jews leave Egypt and bondage. The eleventh plague should have been, was for me, that swarm of aunts, uncles and cousins who buzzed and berated me all week long about my irreligiousness and my congenital impatience, features which made it difficult for me to endure the demands of two marathon Seders. All of my cousins attended the same parochial school in Manhattan and their spring vacation coincided with the Passover holiday whenever it happened to fall. I was in a school that was American enough to fix on Easter as celebratable and permissive enough not to care if a child missed a week of what they gave us as instruction. My mother always said it would be a nice break for me to go with my cousins and that's exactly what it was. They tried to break me and I tried to break away. Both parties succeeded, in part.

The Ostend sat, quite alone, on a stretch of the boardwalk that headed toward Margate and Ventnor and away from the action. The Ostend appeared to be made of yellow brick but up close you could see that it wasn't real brick, just a veneer of what I think was something like tar paper. Inside, the Ostend smelled of old age, mildew, cabbage and Sen-Sen. Everyone sucked Sen-Sen. Either it was specially manufactured for its Orthodox users on Passover or I am misremembering it, slotting that strong odor of my childhood into the wrong place. Sen-Sen came in tin boxes and you had to nudge open one corner of the box so that the tiny black pellets could drop into your hand or on the floor, where a lot of them landed. At the Ostend these pellets were invisible and thus fragrantly irretrievable because all the rugs were black with only occasional red roses in circles on them. Even the sunroom, which doubled as a place of not-so-pagan worship, was carpeted in that ubiquitous black. Upstairs, the tubs had crusty saltwater taps. We were encouraged by our elders to take saltwater baths for our health, although none of us had anything to cure that we knew of. As drafts can kill, the windows at the Ostend were never opened until summertime, which is not when we were there. The windows were, actually, unopenable. They were nailed shut across the sash and weather-stripped with gray felt that kept out the winds and kept in the heat and stink of two hundred or so people eating, gossiping, playing gin rummy, praying, napping and dying. During the times I was at the Ostend, two old women died. They were not friends of my family's, not even acquaintances, so it was exciting. Once a hearse came all the way from Baltimore for the remains, as they called it. Remains: an odd reversal. You would think remains referred to those who lived and not to those who had died.

Most of the hotel's clients were regulars. They came year after year, as did my grandparents and their children, and fussed over changes that were never for the better. The management was of Polish extraction, as were many of the lodgers, although the hotel must have been named for that resort in Belgium that had been my family's preferred watering hole for the last couple of decades before the war that brought them here. That may have been why they went to the Ostend, that and their religion, because they really didn't have much to say to most of the other guests who were, by and large, not even from New York. It helped, naturally, that they had each other to talk to. That family always had each other.

Mrs. Potofsky, the owner's wife, kept a sharp if glaucomatous eye on unnecessary expenditure. Except in the dining room, where she had a reputation to maintain. Lights were dim, cleaning personnel scanty. Children were admitted to the Ostend but not tolerated. Not the

usual club rules: another reversal. On my father's side I
have thirteen cousins and, as no one was yet in college
or still in diapers, all of them were on the premises. The
median age was about my own. Apart from us there were
only a few other children, perhaps a dozen. The atmo-
sphere was definitively geriatric, although I suspect that
in summer it may have been different. There were two
bellboys, also geriatrically inclined, whose chief duty
seemed to be shushing us. We were not, except at meal-
times, to be seen or heard in the salons reserved for adult
pleasures and comforts. Our place was in the basement,
in a room furnished with hundreds of incomplete decks
of cards, the wooden rocking chairs which in summer
were set out on the porch facing the sea, and little else.
On rainy days we rocked like crazy down there, scream-
ing and singing, throwing cards like fistfuls of the sand
it was too wet to play with. Every night at ten, when the
playroom was officially closed, Mrs. Potofsky came down
to make sure that we picked up all the cards and arranged them in neat stacks on the one table.

On fine days we went out. Ostensibly, that's what we
were there for, the air that braced. Passover is a holiday
that lasts eight days but on the middle four days you can
do things, if it isn't the Sabbath, like work or spend
money or ride in a jitney. What we did was go to the Ritz
at my aunt's invitation to swim in the pool with which
their management, not the least bit Polish, saw fit to
furnish a basement. We also rented bikes for rides on the
boardwalk, played on the sand, which at that season felt
like granulated ice, sat on horses that were unwilling to
venture much beyond the Million Dollar Pier where we
hired them and if they did move went right under the
Pier where the waves crashed so fiercely against the
wooden pilings that we wouldn't have any second
thoughts about turning their noses home, and we hit the
penny arcades. Not many of these mechanical palaces
were open before the summer months but when we
rapped hard on the glass doors someone, a caretaker
maybe, usually let us in to lose our nickels and dimes. A

great deal of money passed through our hands in four days. I always ran short and since I didn't like to ask for money, I had to stick to Skee-ball. If you have a steady throwing arm you can score high enough to get coupons that, if you don't want the prizes offered, can get you extra games. I could go for hours on a dollar.

The third year I went to Atlantic City my brother, who had been coughing all winter, was sent along to reap whatever benefits he could from the ocean breezes. He got to stay at the Ritz and of course I never forgave him that. But my brother's being at the Ritz that year had advantages, distinct ones, in the shape of bread and rolls. I happen to dislike matzo almost as much as I dislike being told what and what not to eat. The way matzo sticks to your back teeth and the roof of your mouth in wet lumps is as bad as the way it scratches your throat if you swallow it without chewing it well first, and if you chew it, it sticks and so on. Matzo doesn't provide much in the way of nourishment and it leads to a wide variety of disorders in the lower digestive tract. Not for me, any of it, especially when I had access through my brother to food that didn't fight back. But the real reason I wanted bread was that I had a scheme. I had devised a surefire way to keep from being invited again, ever. I liked Atlantic City all right, for those four days, but I couldn't stand the company. The company couldn't really stand me either and they let me know it, that particular year.

Of the two cousins with whom I shared a room only one, the younger one, who was just a little bit older than I was, had it in for me on general principles. The older girl was already at an age when family can be discounted like certain appliances on a cash-down, no-service, no-returns policy. She couldn't have cared less and didn't. But Debbie, who at thirteen was a candidate for a significant award in maliciousness, I knew would always use her fat mouth to discredit me with the grown-ups. My plan that third Passover was to leave slices of bread and half-eaten rolls in our room to be found and reported on. Such an infraction of every rule would certainly get me sent home and on a permanent basis. Not only was I committing a major personal sin, but by bringing bread into the hotel I was making the entire dwelling unclean and probably uninhabitable. I hoped.

Debbie did her tricks and I was summoned to my aunt's room before dinner on the first day I had left the evidence. In the room were my aunt, my uncle and Mrs. Potofsky. I had figured right. Debbie had squealed not just to her mother but also to the management. I was already dressed for dinner and my knees were shaking so much that the organdy skirt of my dress foamed like the waves I heard outside. From the neck up I was cool, determined not to cry, a paragon. Mrs. Potofsky spoke first, in a voice that was strangely quiet. She was so grief-stricken by the shame and dishonor I had brought to her establishment that, after her opening remarks, her English escaped her and I didn't understand one word of what she said to me. Ten more minutes of this meaning-lessness and she left the room. My uncle left with her. The disciplining of children is a secondary sex character-istic of females and I guess my uncle could not stomach it. My aunt, from whom I expected her customary roars but louder, spoke in nasty sibilant whispers of punish-ments harsher than any she could dish out; judgment, from above, eternal guilt and my habitual inadequacies. All of a sudden I caught on and that's when I started to cry. My aunt and Mrs. Potofsky were going to hush up this whole business and rob me of my way out. Mrs. Po-tofsky must have pleaded with my aunt to consider the greater good of the hotel and its aged inhabitants. My aunt wasn't yelling at me because the walls were thin. I wasn't going to be sent home because, if I were, ques-tions might be asked. Debbie's lips were sealed, I found out later, with the promise of a new tennis racquet and a beating.

III

Impatience is my middle name. That doesn't quite ring like Ishmael's opening remark but neither does my subject measure up to his, and I never had that truculent force, a sweet purity of purpose, that Ishmael makes so much of. What I did have in abundance was a mutinous itch to grow up. I couldn't bear the way the years dawdled by. I was longing to shed the scaly skin that puberty and schooling wrapped so tight around me. If I could have I would have peeled myself older with no concern for any scars that might appear to blemish my adult future.

I don't know now what the big rush was all about because what I saw of the way grown-up women filled their long afternoons didn't look particularly attractive. They had lunches, fittings, nail and hair appointments, lovers, migraines and bridge games, not necessarily in that order. But I suppose it all seemed juicier to me than what I had, which was school, riding, ballet, French tutoring, Hebrew School, speech, visits to my grandparents and the orthodontist, errands and so much more. By eighth grade some homework and a few specific expectations had materialized in school, but after years of floating in that warm sea I was as eager to be told what to do as I was to do it. No great effort was required and I took tests, wrote term papers, thought algebraically, and parsed sentences with a sigh of relief. As grades were not a pertinent feature in a progressive education, I never knew just where I stood. Three of the other girls felt as relieved as I did and we formed a little circle of our own. I was initiated into the ripe mysteries of the telephone, traded I.D. bracelets, and was invited on sleep-overs. I wasn't allowed to go on the sleep-overs very often, so I didn't have what you might call an active social life, but it was a beginning. Schoolwork, lessons and friendships notwithstanding, I still wasn't growing up fast enough. I had to find another way to ease my itch and I did. Two ways, in fact, whose connection escaped me at the time. I started to read and I got fat. I read as sloppily, as voraciously, as I stuffed my mouth, cramming all my abysmal holes. Books and food: twin tits I sucked on, thirsty always. About the books I have little to say. The fat is another story.

For the females in our family, being fat turned out to be a form of cultural conditioning. Every tribe has its *rites de passage,* some more exotic. For my sisters and me, a total immersion in the flesh was the sticky dawn of maturity. After years of having our heads force-fed, our bodies responded in kind, thickening grossly, distending to accommodate the weight of our instructional overload. We blew up: barrage balloons protecting unidentifiable targets from all attackers. When we deflated and our fine bones showed again we were on our own, grown-ups. So simple, although nobody pointed it out to us at the time. If they had, it might all have gone a little faster, more fluently.

My brother never made it. In respect to fat, he resem-

bled my father, who with a narcotic perversity had managed to stay happily obese all of his adult life. Every so
often my father would slough off a few pounds as a
concession to my mother's virulent regime or, perhaps,
out of sentiment. They had met in Marienbad; he on a
reducing cure even then and she there for the vapors
popular that season with young girls looking for hus-
bands. Years later, still dieting, my father would magi-
cally gain back twice what he had given. Sleight of
mouth. It took some doing, for my father never seemed
to eat much at the table. Secret eaters eat secrets.

When I was fat, the dining room was my Waterloo:
every night I fell while my still-skinny little sisters who
had no breasts popped grapes from the centerpiece into
their mouths to mask their snickers. They knew they
would get it from me later if I heard them laughing. My
mother, who had never succeeded in thinning down my
father, decided to do a job on me. Every bite was metered
and if I wanted more what I got was an argument. Inevitably I argued back. Just as inevitably I left the table in
tears, still chewing, choking. I can't remember regularly
finishing dinner in those days. I would lock myself into
my bathroom, dry my tears, and eat the food I had stored
between the folded, never-used towels in the back of the
linen closet. I knew better than to hide food in my room.
We had moved again, in the same building, and I had my
own room now, but there was no lock on the door and it
wasn't a safe place to keep anything. My brother, who
assumed that what I was doing in the bathroom was
crying, felt sorry enough to risk sneaking food into his
pocket which he would then leave under my bed. Why
did he, also fat, get all he wanted to eat at the table? He
never cried or argued, that's true and that's probably it.
Late at night I'd feast again, far under the blankets with
a flashlight, a book and those brotherly leftovers.

To make matters worse, we always had good cooks,
most of whom operated in an ancient tradition of *Schlag*.
Food poured from the kitchen and overwhelmed us

eaters with its rich and persistent interest. When company came, as it did frequently and in very large numbers, we were not seated at the table but in the kitchen instead. A superior place, we thought, in which to observe the steamy chaos that resulted, every time, in orderly spirals of bright food on polished silver platters. One cook had a temper like Torquemada's. She split the air with sharp accusatory bolts of rage at the waitress who was getting in her way, at a sauce that curdled unmercifully, at us watching. Having had enough one night, I stood up to go and, knife in red hand, she charged in my direction. I screamed so loudly that sixteen guests rushed as one into the kitchen. My brother, the twins and the waitress disappeared out the back door. My father stepped forward, the knife dropped, the cook was fired and left on the spot, and I wound up serving the rest of the dinner because the waitress never returned.

There were cooks who drank, cooks who were perilously decrepit, cooks who sometimes let us make a cake on our own for a school bake sale. We once had an American cook who fried everything including tomatoes. She lasted two weeks. The usual turnover was once a year. Because the cooks were generally Hungarian and the waitresses were invariably Irish, communication in the kitchen was on a very primitive level. My mother, on principle, did not mix into the help's business beyond hiring and firing them. So it was often I who was called into the kitchen to act as interpreter and mediator, although Hungarian was not a language I had. For these services, if successfully performed that is, I was assured of at least a week's worth of heads averted when I slipped into the kitchen to steal food for my cache in the closet. My brother stole money from my father's handkerchief drawer to buy candy on Columbus Avenue, but I never had the nerve to steal anything that wasn't already paid for.

Stealing food was as much of an enterprise as eating it. I had to plan carefully, thinking about spoilage and detectability, plotting my future appetites. The food at school, mostly cheesy, was not worth lifting, so my entire hoard had to be gathered at home. Since I was out of the house every day until close to dinnertime, when the kitchen was busiest, I stole primarily on weekends, at night and on vacations. Occasionally, late at night in the dark kitchen, I'd bump into my father or my brother, all of us barefoot for the stealthiest purposes. I never bought food in a store because I needed my allowance to pay for the movies I saw, surreptitiously, on weekends when I could steal the time. Stealing time, stealing food, I was a plundering, ponderous glutton.

Round and surrounded: the geometry of my circumscription. I wore garter belts and Kotex belts, mental chastity belts (as if I needed one!), cinch belts and silver bangles, circle pins and circle skirts. I was as loopy as those cloth and metal hoops around me and my limbs, a teenager with a mouth as big as her ass. My skin was clear, my hair paged just so, my teeth as straight as my nose, but was I fat. The day I outweighed my mother by twenty pounds was the day we paid a visit to Madame Tina, ex-Antwerp, a sorcerous corsetiere on upper Broadway who cast her spells in a shop you had to be slim to fit into. Grown-up underwear, it seemed, was not bought in department stores but made *sur mesure*. I knew this was only a way of saying that my particular measurements were too abnormal for ordinary life.

Madame Tina was the only person besides my pediatrician who ever took a good look at what I myself would not examine. She clucked and prodded and measured and, in ten days, created an arrangement in elastic, rubber and lace punctuated with zippers and hooks and eyes. This ferocious apparatus was stiff enough to sit up by itself and was designed to make me conform to a perfect ladies' size sixteen dress. My mother refused to buy anything larger; it was sixteen or go naked. So I wore the corset. I even came to like the whooshing noise I made when I sat down too fast and air rushed out through the tiny holes of the elastic. Everywhere that edge met flesh there would be a roll under my clothes. I walked slowly so that the rolls wouldn't wobble. My posture certainly improved in that harness. I was not the only fat girl in school. My friend Anya was even fatter than I was but that's not the reason she was my best friend. A few of the boys were fat. But I was constricted and they were all free and it made a big difference.

There were other shops we went to on upper Broadway. Buying shoes at Indian Walk was the closest I came to aboriginal America for decades. We'd go to Rappaport's for sporting goods and our camp clothes. We bought blue jeans there but I wasn't permitted to wear them except when I was in camp and invisible. We went to a notions store for buttons, ribbons, velvet rickrack and all the other trimmings that my mother tacked on to clothes she was tired of and could possibly transform for me. And, just off Broadway in a tiny basement, there was Lola, also ex-Antwerp, a formerly grand lady whose livelihood now was making chocolates. I was sent once a month to pick up our portion. Lola could make very little candy and would sell only to people she knew well. I'd ring her bell and wait for the long time it took for her to trudge from the stove to the door. Lola always quizzed me about my father's family so that she could make sure I was who I said I was. She never seemed to recognize me from month to month. A crowd of kettles bubbled on a black stove and there were piles of nuts, raisins and orange peels on the floor beside the stove. Lola's arms to the elbows were covered with melted chocolate as she wrapped one pound, her limit to any customer, in a box. She never let me taste even a dripping from her arm. I'd steal just one chocolate from the box on the way home. I could not take more because my mother knew exactly what a pound consisted of.

For really serious shopping we went downtown twice a year. The wide aisles of Best's, De Pinna's, Saks' and Bendel's resounded with our passage, for me never triumphant. In each store my mother had a saleswoman who knew her all too well. My favorite was Miss Mildred,

at Bendel's, so that's where we went most often. Miss
Mildred had a daughter my age who during school vacations came to the store with her mother and sat reading
in the stockroom. I remember that my mother once invited this girl to join us for lunch at Rumpelmayer's but
she didn't want to come. Dresses, suits, coats and school
clothes would be heaped high in the dressing room and
we concentrated on dark clothes to minimize my critical
mass. I had, fortunately and with some help from Madame Tina, a smallish waist and we tried to make the
most of it. I trusted Miss Mildred's Ohioan eye. I'd put on
one piece of clothing after another, avoiding a look in the
three-way mirror. Eventually, a few things would fit and
I'd have a new wardrobe. I looked just fine, Miss Mildred
said, just fine, honey.

For many years my father had a deaf and dumb tailor.
The tailor came to our house in the evenings quite regularly, grunting, chalky-fingered, his valise packed with
pale muslin patterns stitched and penciled. Of course I
couldn't watch my father's fittings but I saw the tailor
come and go and deliver jackets and pants and coats
whose variety was rarely discernible to the naked eye.
He suited my father, I thought, in more ways than one.
And if there were such a thing as a blind tailor, my father
might have hired him as well. That's not as snide as it
sounds. I'm sure my father welcomed, as we all did, a
moment of respite from the continuous onslaught of my
mother's loquacity and sharp-sightedness.

The only time our house was really silent, and unnat-
urally so, was when my mother had her monthly migraines. On migraine days we were as considerate and
as mute as the radios my father made us turn off. Otherwise, we were not either of these things to each other. In
spite of those clockwork headaches my mother would
usually attempt the dinner table. Wan and nauseous,
fretful, sort of floating in her loose dressing gown, she
would take one look at the food on her plate, roll her eyes,

and make straight for the dark of her bed. In my parents'
bedroom there were heavy black curtains sewn onto the
backs of the more conventionally colored drapes that
crossed, at night, each window. Lightproof. That's the
word and that was the intention. I knew even then that
there's more to lightproofing than what meets the eye,
that marriage is a shady business. Once, my brother and
sisters and I had measles together and we managed
without difficulty to infect my mother and the maid. We
had to spend the daylight hours on cots in my parents'
black bedroom to soothe our photophobia. My father
stayed home for a day or two and nursed us all gently, as
carefully as he could in the dark. Lampless and sound-
less, my father moved in that room through the dooms of
his inexpressible love for us.

My mother never had any trouble expressing herself. A
nonstop talker, she was like a deluxe train, a *rapido*.
Glittering with brightwork and vividly plush, she sped
from subject to subject without pausing to let passengers
on. Her trips could be instructive, entertaining, exhaust-
ing or irritating, depending on your view out of any particular window, and they were frequently all of these at
once. Talkers who listen are your great talkers. That's
called conversation. We didn't have too much of it at
home, although when there was company we would
overhear intricate anecdotes about, say, my parents' life
in the Far East for several years before my birth. The
relative merits of haberdashery by Sulka or Knize was
another regular subject of conversation, as were government subsidy of the opera, Zionism and summer travel
plans. My parents had a small entourage of politically
questionable acquaintances for a while in the fifties, in
our house by dint of my mother's dominant persuasions,
and blacklisting replaced Bangkok as a dinner-table
topic. So conversation was possible, it just wasn't for
children. We were treated instead to verbal harassment
from the distaff side. Being truly her children, we ha-
rassed right back but our counterattacks never seemed

to get us anywhere. We were either wrong or wronged, and neither condition provided much in the way of advancement or satisfaction.

The issues are unclear now, the enemies and outcome dubious, but we really did wage war at the time. Our best fights were fought in the dining room. Noisy, impassioned and illogical, our strategies hovered and conjoined in that room that smelled perpetually, delightfully, of goulash. The polished mahogany table winked as encouragingly as the waitress who served us and we fought and fought and always surrendered, but not in peace and quiet. My father, like a deskbound General, oversaw the action from afar. I was in the thick of it, leading my brother and sisters into the kind of combat that they, leaderless, could certainly have avoided. I don't mean to say we were always fighting, my mother and I. Much of the time we weren't even speaking and much of the rest of the time I was all too ready to accept my mother's estimation of my insufficiencies. What a chump I must have been! In spite of our mutual and trashy arrogance, clearly a gift from her father to both of us, it was always *me* on the defensive. That's a difficult line to hold, more difficult to abandon.

I fought for some foolish things like lipstick and curfews and Tampax and black turtleneck sweaters and going to school on Yom Kippur. The larger battles all centered, I felt, on my being an American in a family that went west only to get to the Hudson River where the boats that took them to Europe every summer were docked. Some American. I had one foot forward and the other foot planted firmly and possibly forever in the rich mud of another country, in another time. I didn't even have my own naturalization papers. What I had was "derivative" citizenship, stemming from my father's papers, although surely my derivation, like his, was elsewhere. A black-robed judge swore us in one morning in my fourteenth year. I went downtown with my parents, excused from school but assigned to give a report in assembly on my swearing-in. Shuffling documents like a canasta deck, listening to me pledge allegiance to a flag that stood beside his high desk, the judge said I would never need more than what he gave to me that day. He was mistaken.

One day my uncle, the misfit, went mad. He had shock treatments and died soon after. This happened when I was sixteen, an adolescent oyster internally secreting what I hoped would be a pretty pearly self. I don't want to sound off too loud about my uncle's death but I have to say that it was for me the basis of an *entente* I made with my amazing itch and the behavior it had provoked. Not a treaty, just an *entente*, and it wasn't a very cordial one.

I never knew precisely the cause of what they called my uncle's depression. I hadn't, since those early days in my grandparents' living room, been very close to my uncle although he had always been a favorite uncle. After he died I remembered that he had announced Roosevelt's death to us one day when we were in Lake Placid, rushing up Fawn Hill with his arms full of newspapers. And I remembered that I sat on the stone porch steps of our house and watched my uncle slowly, surgically, tear those newspapers into narrow strips and stuff them into his mouth, his pockets, his shoes, all his personal cavities, as if ingestion would ensure digestion. Another dream? Roosevelt died in April and we wouldn't have been in Lake Placid then.

A year before my uncle's death I was a bulky, sulky bridesmaid at his oldest daughter's wedding, tricked out in a green that did little but compete with my complexion. My uncle led me once or twice around the dance floor and that was as near as I ever got to him. An affectionate smile had settled on his face and would not be dislodged by anything I said because he was by then more deaf than hearing, distanced by his infirmity, perhaps. The room in which the wedding took place was on the roof of a grand hotel. The ceiling soared, arched high above us like a domed and dazzling railway station. I was a little drunk. Many languages clattered in an air scented with thousands of flowers at their peak. People danced around us as if they were travelers rushing to make trains, bounding and stomping their Jewish dance steps, white handkerchiefs waving goodbye. I lost my uncle in the bustle. When I heard, eavesdropping on my parents late one night, about my uncle's shock treatments, I couldn't help making the Froeschmann connection, an electric bond between us.

I was reading the Russians at the time. Tolstoy, Gogol, Dostoevski, Turgenev: the Princess and my friend Anya may have predisposed me to these dark fictions but they hardly prepared me for how my uncle fit in, right into the teeth of thundering catastrophe and desolation. Maybe my uncle, more of a prince to me than Myshkin ever was, gave in at long last, outcast, to the lean and rigid togetherness of a family that didn't want any part of him. Or was it that he didn't give in? Giving in, giving up, getting out: there's a thin fabric of grace and favor in our lives that can be stretched just so far before it rips and you with it. I couldn't let that first snag appear that would end, I knew it, with me in shreds, snarled and uncontrollable.

There was a game we used to play when I was younger, called "blindsies," hopscotch with your eyes closed. You could look to see where your stone or the skate key we often played with had landed. After that initial peek it was instinct, memory and an inner balance that mattered if you wanted to win. The *entente* I made was a version of blindsies. I decided that the mind, boxwise, has thick flaps of feeling you can glue shut if you want to, when you need to. Blindsies. I didn't have to feel everything and the waiting would not chafe me. I gave up my lessons. I gave up culture and refinement. I gave up the care and feeding of that pearly secretion. At home I practiced a vile and disobedient silence. Finally, I stopped fighting. Finally, I stopped eating.

IV

I found *ma semblable, ma soeur,* one weekend in Lakewood, New Jersey, when I was fifteen and needed a *semblable* in the worst way. Anya, Annushka, whom I had known for most of my sentient life and had categorically avoided. Anya and I started in the first grade together at The Walden School. From that day on, when we discovered that we were both French-speaking, we did not really speak until the weekend in Lakewood many years later. We discovered we both spoke French (information like that would have never crossed *my* lips except in the form of an accent I couldn't control) when the teacher made a big production out of it. She told all the other children to speak to us V* E* R* Y slowly. She also threw in a gratuitous dissertation on the War and its refugees. What those children understood, of course, was that we were the enemy, promptly to be fought. First graders are nothing if not physical and by the end of the week I had been bitten, scratched and punched into total surrender. Anya, a screamer, suffered fewer bruises because of the shrill alarms she sounded whenever anyone approached her. It was much better, safer, not to acknowledge each other's existence. Our mothers met, early on, and ritual invitations to birthday parties were issued for several years. They made no serious attempt to bring us together fearing, as they should have, to compound our difficulties.

Anya's parents were *émigrés* on another, more exotic axis. They came at one time from Russia, had both been educated and orphaned in Palestine, and had been living in Paris, where Anya was born, when the War broke out. I could never get the story straight enough to make much sense of it, because Anya and her mother were compulsive embellishers and her father was the silent type. Mr. Marshall (his name had been anglicized in Palestine by Britishers who couldn't work their long teeth around a Russian patronymic) was an engineer. He had been working for ten years on an invention that would, in another few years, make him a very rich man. But they came to New York as penniless as they had been in Paris.

Anya lived with her parents on the third floor of a brownstone around the corner from us. If they were as poor as my mother said, it wasn't too bad. Anya's mother rented movies for her parties. What I had was our governess supervising her unique version of pin the tail on the donkey, which involved tiny flags on pins and a map of Europe. Whoever got closest to Antwerp, in my honor on my birthday, won. Educational, always. Anya's velvet party dresses had enormous lace collars on them, hanging almost halfway down her back. I knew that was the mark of a really expensive party dress. Of scholarships, sacrifices and debts I knew nothing. I remember only one room in Anya's house, from those birthdays. There was a big piano standing in a corner. Mrs. Marshall was a pianist who had, as she was later to tell me, over and over, given up a promising career (references from Nadia Boulanger available upon request) when she gave birth to Anya. With no money to pay for a nurse, she had no time to continue with her musical studies. Mrs. Marshall always played volcanic accompaniments to the silent films unreeling on the screen before us. It was a small room and by the end of the afternoon we were deaf and glassy-eyed, overcome and overfed, exhausted.

Anya went her way and I went mine. We saw each other every day in school and were as evasive of one another as was possible in a class that numbered twenty-two, give or take a few over the years. I assumed, not really caring, that her childhood was an easier one than mine, which was turning out to be more of a tightrope act than anything else. My assumption about Anya was based on the observation that she laughed a lot and was undeniably popular. Boys and girls rushed to take her hand when we had to form lines to cross the street into the park for sports. Anya always had money in her pockets and would buy candy for her friends of the week from the old man who came to stand on the corner with his pushcart at three o'clock when we were dismissed. With her thick black hair and chalky skin, her blue eyes, the general configuration of her nose, brows and teeth, Anya was a potential stand-in for Elizabeth Taylor as she appeared in *National Velvet,* a favorite film. When we did a play, Anya often got the lead. If it was a musical, she always got it. In many respects she reminded me of my brother, who occupied the same sort of position one class below us that Anya did in ours. I really didn't care.

Soon Mr. Marshall managed to get some backing and began to manufacture his invention, a gadget which revolutionized submarine steering mechanisms, if I understood it right. During the year we were in sixth grade, Anya and her parents moved to a large apartment on Central Park South. A brother was born: wonderfully ignorable at our advanced age. In a short time, Mr. Marshall was well on his way to becoming an important man with government contracts, multiple factories, Cadil-

lacs, Chinese houseboys and country properties rapidly
snowballing. The glamorous details of this prototypical
New World success story were aired and examined daily
in the middle school lunchroom by Anya and her friends,
whose interest in that story and the goods that money
provides was not particularly sociological. The lunchroom was located just off a balcony that ran around the
second story of the gymnasium, all of it underground and
windowless. The balcony was used as an indoor track,
and high-school runners had a regular practice during
our lunch period. Each lap resounded, shook up the stew
and rattled the Jell-O and made mush, as Anya's brag-
ging did, of my stomach. Would I ever catch up? Not to
win, just to run in the great American race was goal
enough.

In Lakewood, then, I was *au courant* if not exactly in
the mainstream of Anya's life. On a rainy Friday during
our Easter vacation, with more rain forecast for the
weekend, some other girl or perhaps several of them
must have let Anya down. Her mother called mine and
arrangements were made to which I must have con-
sented although I can't imagine doing so. Anya was in
Lakewood with her father, who had been closeted all
week with some scientists, a few financiers and a couple
of Navy officials in a remote and rather primitive hotel
in the middle of a pinewoods. The expression "think
tank" wasn't yet in the vocabulary but I suppose that's
what was going on in that incongruous setting. Why the
tank wasn't located at the Marshalls' country house was
forever a mystery to me. Anya's mother had been sick,
unable to join the group as hostess before the weekend,
and she said that Anya was anxious for some company
out there. She picked me up before lunch. The limousine,
the chauffeur, the rain on the windows, Mrs. Marshall's
Russified French, which I had trouble understanding: it
was all better than any movie until I got out of the car
and saw the look on Anya's face. She hadn't been expect-

ing me, not at all. I was the surprise her mother had mentioned on the telephone. It was a fragile moment. Anya had great style, even then. She rose above her disappointment with a flourish. In a bravura performance she welcomed me to Lakewood and took me up to the first of many rooms we would share.

What happened was that we played true confessions most of the weekend. For me it was a grand new game. I found a sister, far superior to the ones I had left at home. Some doors opened. I fell in love. Things go fast when you're fifteen and there isn't much time.

Clearing up all previous business took about eight hours. We talked late into Friday night and agreed that our avoidance had been mutually necessary. Anya claimed I had no right, never having been poor myself, to question her use and maybe abuse of money. I conceded that point, somewhat apologetically. She said that her socializing in school was a sham, a deliberate act of assimilation on her part, signifying nothing. That one was more difficult to swallow but I did it, seeing as how it brought her closer to the view I wanted to have of her. In a ceremony for which we were really too old but which we enjoyed immensely, we fingerprinted each other's diaries in blood. Together, different, the same, we would conquer. To seal our bond Anya gave me a gift, a crack at a college-boy waiter, dark and delicious (I had already noticed him at dinner), whom she had been warming up all week. I gave her my mind, the promise of it, after she admitted that she hadn't read much beyond *Daddy Long-Legs* and had found herself unable to make the kind of conversation she needed to make to impress the boys she wanted to impress. And the Latin homework, please! We both knew it was an even exchange and one with a future.

On Saturday Anya and I lingered intolerably in the dining room, sitting at the breakfast and lunch table long after the Marshalls and assorted brains had left. The waiter waited, as he was meant to do. We drank cup after

cup of tea to justify our presence, trying to disregard the
effect all that tea was producing on our bladders. Roger,
so named by his parents and by the green disc pinned to
his lapel, finally sat down with us after dinner at the very
moment that I had to excuse myself or flood the chair. I
never knew what Anya said to him while I was gone but
when I came back Roger asked if we wanted to go for a
walk after he had finished in the kitchen. We accepted.
We were to meet him in ten minutes by the garages.
When we got there Anya put on another star performance. Her mother forbade her, absolutely forbade her,
to go out, she was being punished and so on. A nice set-
up. It was too dark to see Roger's expression and I didn't
mind if he minded or not.

It was still raining, more mist than drop. I had on
Anya's trench coat: my own rain gear was hopelessly
childish, a yellow hooded slicker. Roger told me he was
at Bowdoin (I hadn't actually heard of it), an English
major, taking a year off, trying to write, getting nowhere
with it, it being a novel. Incredible! Thank you, Anya,
spasiba, and for not telling me. I felt as if I were walking
through a scenario which only I could have written for
myself, it was that perfect. I managed to work a phrase
from "Prufrock" into my end of the conversation (a de-
mented teacher had pointed me in Eliot's direction only
the week before), hoping that would do the job. It seemed
to. We talked books in the rainy woods for two hours and
on the way back Roger held my hand. I was very large
for my age, which of course I had lied about anyway. I
stumbled. I knew every trick in the book, even if I hadn't
used them before. His arms went out to catch me. Face,
up. Kiss? Cut! Print.

I passed many hours on Sunday morning drafting what
turned out to be an exquisite letter to Roger. I planned to
give it to him as we left to go back to New York. It wasn't
the sort of hotel that provides either stationery or writing
tables for its guests in their rooms. Not wanting to use
the paper that Anya got from her father, with a big "Mar-

shall Products" on it, I wrote on the shelf paper that lined the bureau drawers, sprawled on the cold linoleum floor. The paper was glossy on both sides and my pen skidded over it, making what I had to say more or less illegible. Anya copied what she could read of my drafts. She wanted to use them, she said, whenever the occasion arose. I told her it was silly, I could write her letters any time, but she insisted on keeping her copies. They were a record, she said, a token of my first infatuation. Anya herself was a veteran infatuate. I explained that Roger wasn't quite first. I had liked a boy that winter, the older brother of a girl in our class, but he hadn't liked me back. And what, Anya said, was a boy next to Roger!

Roger hadn't appeared on Sunday's breakfast shift. At lunch, our last meal there, he was waiting on tables at the other end of the dining room and he did not speak to us. I gave my letter to the desk clerk, a smarmy type, who assured me that he would get it to Roger all right. We left shortly after lunch. For the next two months until school ended, Anya and I ran across the street to my house every day at eleven, before Biology, to check the mail before the elevator man took it upstairs. I never did hear from Roger but it hardly mattered. I had, now, some experience that was more mine and real than what I had encountered on celluloid and in print. It seemed to be a workable model. And I also had a sister.

I spent that summer in Switzerland at the pension for young ladies that I attended for several summers after I outgrew the athletic camps that are such a heavy industry in the Maine woodlands. I was being finished for what I sincerely hoped was the last time. Anya was on a kibbutz near the Delaware Water Gap for six weeks. In spite of their shiny new money and Mr. Marshall's sensitive manufactural position, the politics practiced in that household were irredeemably Socialist. The notion of a kibbutznik arriving in a limousine didn't faze either the Marshalls or Anya in the slightest. They had developed an attitude of fiscal indifference that they quite casually projected onto the rest of the world; money was never more than a convenience for them. After the summer, I was invited almost every weekend to the Marshalls' house on the North Shore of Long Island. My mother let me accept about once a month. I suppose my parents suddenly realized that college was only two years away and that they had better begin to let go, in a physical sense at any rate.

The house was vast: brown shingles above fieldstone walls and porches. On a hill, it had a view of the Sound. It possessed the disreputable ghost of a previous owner whose death by drowning (?) was still the scandal of Lloyd Harbor. There was an orchard, the requisite gardens, stables, dogs, Ping-Pong tables and in the library a mint collection of *Esquire*s, bought along with the house, which I devoured. The house was filled on weekends with scientists, pipe-smokers all, and young male musicians, usually Israeli (that country had long had its new name), whose education Mrs. Marshall was sponsoring at one conservatory or another on the Eastern seaboard. Besides myself there was another regular, Mr. Marshall's private secretary-cum-lawyer, a small man with a round and red face whom I took at first for a valet, so obsequiously did he talk to the boss. He didn't come often to the table, mealtime being his typing time, so that notes of the conversations would be ready for the scientists, who did nothing but converse between meals. Anya and I had to share the musicians with Mrs. Marshall, who kept them playing duets in the music room for interminable hours. I knew by now all about her ex-career but I couldn't really forgive her for the way she made those hopefuls sing for their supper. Anya's brother, rarely seen indoors irrespective of the weather, was the only person who, when his nanny allowed it, could tempt Mrs. Marshall away from the piano. It was never often enough for Anya and me.

Those weekends were instant asylum for me, both

madhouse and sanctuary. It was a world of Stashas and
Volodyas, of loud voices and louder music, of *"chérie,
veux-tu dire à Annushka que son cheval est prêt?"* of
pauses at the dinner table during which people actually
reflected on what had just been said. It was so like the
Chekhov I was reading that I listened at night for the
thumping stick of the watchman and I swear I sometimes heard it. Columbus in reverse, I was discovering a
possible Europe, one unfettered by family and obligations. At the same time, at home, I was exploring America. Gross confusion, as usual, resulted. Anya had much
less ambivalence than I did. Her parents were so permissive, as soft as the jam they spooned into their tea, that
she never equated Europe with severity.

I guess I sang for my supper too. Not very profession-
ally, as the musicians did, but in another way. I was an
"influence," supposed to keep Anya reading and her
schoolwork up to par, and above all to keep her from
indulging what was considered her unfortunate interest
in young men, of whom there were several on the premises in the shape of part-time stableboys and gardener's
assistants. Mrs. Marshall spelled all this out for me one
morning when Anya, who slept later than I could, was
upstairs. The musicians being her business, Mrs. Marshall didn't mention them. For a minute I thought I
hadn't understood her, that odd French again, but of
course I had. I could hardly tell her that not only was she
too late but that the last thing I wanted to be was what
she took me for, so I told her what she wanted to hear,
that I would do my best. It was the first secret I kept from
Anya since Lakewood, which wasn't right because she
had shared such a really good one with me when she got
back from the kibbutz. Anya had, on a blanket in a tomato field one night at the end of August, lost her virginity. As she told it I could see clearly the glorious red pool
of blood and tomato pulp; oh, the smell of it, the juice of
it, the lumps and bumps of it. I could have killed Roger
for my deprivation.

The year went by, long and contradictory as those
years were. Anya and I were as close as two people fun-
damentally unsuited to one another can be. Of course we
weren't, or maybe we wouldn't be, aware of any such
incompatibility then. I continued to go on those weekends and by sheer determination taught myself to sleep
later. To sleep a great deal, in fact. What with all that
lying in bed on weekends and various other things at
home—the shocking death of my uncle for one—I got
thinner, thin. As I lost weight so did Anya. Anya's tomato
masher lived in Hackensack, not too far away, and he
was on her mind when not on her belly. I slept. She made
love. It wasn't fair.

What was even more unfair was that Anya began, by
the time senior year started, to tell her mother, on occasional week nights, that she was staying over at my
house. I had my own phone in my room (correction: the
phone was for all four children but it was in my room—
work that one out equably; we never could), so when
Mrs. Marshall called it was me to whom she spoke and
not to my mother. She may have had some thoughts
about why Anya spent so much of her time at our house
in the bathroom but she never voiced them. I had Anya's
boyfriend's number so I could call to tell her to call her
mother back. I lied more for Anya than I ever could for
myself. I'm a lousy liar and I didn't like it. But Anya did
stay overnight from time to time. That was the year my
mother had hired a cook who was profoundly committed
to hollandaise sauce, which appeared on the table in a
sauce boat practically every evening with little regard
for what else was on the menu. Now that I no longer ate,
it didn't bother me. Anya at our dinner table charmed my
parents, my sisters and especially my brother with her
flashy laughter and her unbelievable imitations. Anya
could do a Peter Lorre, a Baby Snooks, a Tallulah, like
nobody else I knew. We all rolled off our chairs in the
proverbial manner, dissolved in high-pitched hysteria,

which was a habitual mood in our house although generally arrived at in another fashion. On a few of the nights Anya stayed I wrote all of her college applications for her and I *know* my essay got her into Sarah Lawrence.

I had a boyfriend of my own that year, although he was not in any Hackensackian sense a lover. An oboist, Paolo had been teaching at the co-ed arts camp on Cape Cod that I had stamped my foot about and been allowed to attend, sore-legged but triumphant, the summer before. Anya had spent a second summer on the kibbutz and was not able to persuade me to join her. I wanted to act with a capital A, no question about it. Paolo lived in Pittsburgh and I was conducting what amounted to a correspondence course in Love with him. I never got that diploma. Paolo was not Italian, or at least not for the last two generations, but he had chosen to use that version of his name thinking it would advance his career, the musical world being what it was then. He played with the Pittsburgh Symphony, second desk, which was pretty good for someone his age, ten years older than mine. Tall, sensual (as far as I could tell), talented: everything I always wanted in a man. Paolo had quite literally swept me up and away, off a tennis court, when to my amazement I won the camp tournament and in leaping across the net fell flat on my face. Along with music Paolo taught tennis, but he had never paid much attention to me until that moment when, coated with red clay, sweat, pride and embarrassment, I cried in his arms. It was, as such tournaments are, near the end of the summer. The following and final days were a week-long sneak preview of coming attractions that never arrived.

The faculty were not supposed to fraternize in any intimate way with the campers for the obvious reasons of which I was a perfect example. Mrs. Grant, the iron-haired virago who ran the camp and whose primary qualification for so doing was that she had once been a member of the Old Vic company, understudy to the stars, was very explicit about that from the start. We had all, girls outnumbering boys by about five to one, heard the sad and pointed story of a beautiful young dancer who years before, out of unrequited love for the ballet master, had thrown herself down from the steep cliff above the beach. She was now a cripple, her career wrecked on those sandy shores. It would have been much saner and probably cheaper for Mrs. Grant to hire only women teachers, but I think the fact that she had two unmarried and overripe daughters who worked in the camp office had something to do with the happy abundance of male instructors.

Paolo and I could meet only at night, inquisitive and accusative eyes being too much a part of the daylight hours. The beach was out, as Mrs. Grant's cottage was perched right at the top of the stairs that provided the only sensible means of access to the water. We met in the woods, piney, Rogerish at first but not for long. On the third night Paolo took off my clothes, strictly from the waist up, and did things to my breasts with his mouth that gave us both some pleasure and some pain. He had a "problem," he said, with my virginity. I had a problem with it too, which was in no way resolvable until he dealt positively with his problem first. With only three nights left I didn't think our problems were going to make it and they didn't.

We corresponded. I wrote endless, mindless letters, addressed to a post-office box number, which Anya transcribed almost verbatim and sent off to Hackensack between visits. Paolo rarely wrote back but he called frequently. I never called him because although I had the phone I wasn't paying the bills. In April the Pittsburgh came to play one concert at Carnegie Hall. My parents, whose regular subscriptions were to the Philharmonic and the Philadelphia, couldn't understand my wish to hear such an inferior orchestra. It was the *Symphonie Fantastique*, I said, which I simply had to hear live. For the week before the concert I feigned a passion for Berlioz, playing two records of his music over and over. It was a stiff pain. I went with Anya on a Wednesday night and saw Paolo on stage. His black hair glistened under the lights. In a tailcoat he looked older than I remembered him. After the concert Anya and I went to the performers' greenroom. The orchestra was going back by bus to Pittsburgh right after the concert and there was no chance of any time alone. Paolo promised to come to New York in June, a special present for my graduation. I began to suspect that he had a little wife tucked away in a little house on a sooty little street. Anya thought he was divine, a real dish, but cruel in his eyes. Anya and I were accomplished analysts of the looker-into-eyes variety.

One effect of Paolo's presence in my head, if not exactly in my day-to-day, was that I didn't have too much interest in the local talent that was by now beginning to knock frequently on a door I wasn't quite desperate enough to open to them. Men only: no classmates need apply. At an age when being sophisticated looked like a life's work, Anya and I were trying to get a head start. We went to a Times Square beauty shop and had our hair straightened (regrettably), wore sunglasses at all times except during basketball practice, used cigarette holders, and spoke nothing but French to each other in the student lounge at school. Being fluent in another language was now a badge of honor, certifiable by College Board scores. We read *Bonjour, Tristesse* and it became our bible and battle cry, even though Anya was getting it regularly and I couldn't see that she had too much to be *triste* about. Existentialism, a mean and mighty wind, hit Central Park West and blew us both eastward, backward to the Paris of Anya's birth and my speculations. For a while that year I listed Continentally.

Letters of acceptance came in May from all the colleges to which I had applied. I chose Wellesley because it seemed to offer an education so opposite to the one I had been getting that it had to be right for me. And I wanted to head north, like Stuart Little, to a more indigenous and obvious America, having as that spry mouse did many reasons to get away from New York and none to stay. June came and Paolo didn't. I commenced.

V

My mother was a sensational dancer. In a class with Adele Astaire and Eleanor Powell, I thought, based on the old movies I saw on television and at the Modern. My mother even used to look like Adele Astaire, black hair swung down in flat S-curves over the tops of her ears, until she decided one day when I was about ten that there was something in those Clairol ads after all. But when she danced, blonde or whatever, she danced like a brunette, which is to say warmly, without agitation. Her arms looked as if they were suspended in a sling of thinnest air, all round and angleless, her back straight or arched as the music and fashion demanded, her head dipped to one side, her legs and feet on invisible ball bearings that glided without friction across any floor, on her face the smile that only total competence, total control can smile.

I rarely saw my father dance with my mother until I was older, at charity balls like the Blind Dance and the Blood Dance, malfunctions all. At home, sometimes, we had dancing and deportment lessons after an occasional

dinner during which we all indulged in food and not in
fight. In a benign mood, we'd get up from the table and
roll up one corner of the large Chinese rug in the living
room. Then my mother and my father would demon-
strate steps to the four of us, my brother and sisters and
me. My brother and I were adamant in our refusal to go
to dancing school and we had to learn sometime, that
was the theory. In practice it didn't quite work out that
way, for reasons which surely had to do with impossible
records and a terrible lack of tenacity on everybody's
part. My twin sisters danced, hopped really, together. My
brother danced with my mother and I with my father. In
spite of his considerable girth my father was very light
on his feet. As I was, am, a stumbler it made for a certain
disjunction in our movement always. My parents' specialty was the tango as it was danced in Marienbad in
1933, a difficult little number involving a lot of midair
swooping and snapping around of heads led by chins. If
we could learn that tango, we could cope with anything
that a dance floor and polite society could come up with.
Wrong again. Elvis was already out there honking a pre-
lude to the kind of music that was to make tangos and
society obsolete before we mastered them, or didn't, as I
couldn't.

The way I knew about my mother being a dancer was
that, as oldest, I sometimes got to go on vacation with
her in February to Palm Beach, a garden spot my father
does not tolerate and therefore does not visit. We always
stayed in a hotel called the Whitehall, which is now a
museum like my memory of it. The Whitehall had been
built by a Mr. Flagler to house his pretensions and it did
some job. I loved it. It was like staying in a picture book
and I was that young duchess descending the grand double staircase. I was usually the only young duchess
around because the week we went, in high season, was
not normally considered vacation time by the academic
establishment. I can't imagine why my mother took me
along. I couldn't have been very endearing company for

her in those years we went, when I was a rude and misanthropical adolescent. I might have legitimized my presence and her trip if I had been ill, chronically coughing or rasping, but I was a girl on the good side of healthy.

In Palm Beach at the Whitehall and now, I suppose, under a different name in a very different sort of place, there existed a breed of great-looking men known as dancing teachers. The Whitehall had at least half a dozen of them on tap. Of course they were gigolos, even I knew that, and I have to say I never saw a gigolo whose looks I didn't like although the tennis pros were more my type. For a fee, these men taught you to dance the latest dance. Other services they performed for another fee. The dancing part worked something like this. At cocktail dances and after-dinner dances they would come up to a table at which few or no men were seated and ask a lady for a dance. In one short spin they got close enough to make suggestions of an educational or that other nature. If they happened across a woman like my mother, who was a really accomplished dancer, they would dance with her often so as to show the uninitiated what was in store for them. As I sat at my mother's table, once a night they had to ask me to dance even though I made it clear from the beginning that I wasn't going to take any lessons. The rest of those evenings I watched my mother glimmer and liquefy in the arms of one gorgeous man after another, wondering what those conversations could be about. I'd work my way through three ginger ales, my limit, making them last until eleven, when I was sent to bed. How long they danced I did not know because being healthy often means that you sleep soundly. The other place I saw my mother do her stuff was in verandah grills on the several Atlantic crossings that we made together. Again, my father did not accompany us on these trips. He would fly over to join my mother in Switzerland or Italy somewhere but he did not cross by boat with us, and I never saw my father in a verandah grill.

Verandah grill. Verandah grill. I grew up in a verandah grill, became a woman in a verandah grill. Not precisely in the grill itself but in a situation that arose out of
a conversation about Yale and man one night in a verandah grill. It wasn't just trial by repartee. Verandah
grill. I could repeat the words one hundred times today
and they would still grab me, trip me up and back like
Proust's cobblestones or his dry fluted cakes. I say verandah grill and other loaded words follow, a little roll
call. *Mauretania, Aquitania, Imperator, Bremen, Ile de
France, De Grasse, Normandie, Queen Mary, Queen
Elizabeth, Constitution, Nieuw Amsterdam, Andrea
Doria.* Some sunk, some shelled, some scuttled, most
scrapped and mostly before my time. But I traveled on
four of them, once as an infant coming over, which is
enough to make the names alone of those liners buzz in
my head, a verbal appliance short-circuiting, spinning
me off into a world of Blue Ribbon races, of Atlantic
crossings and comings of age, of verandah grills. Sleek,
slick, classy verandah grills and their French Line equiv-
alents, my mother's turf.

Abaft, aloft, amazing verandah grill. On the *Queen
Mary* the grill was wrapped around by tall narrow windows that gave out onto terraced decking down to the
backwash. On ships as on land, you often get the best
view with your back turned to the business at hand,
which in this instance was getting to Europe in early
July of the summer before I started college. At lunch-
time, the sun such as it is on the North Atlantic run
flooded the grill with a glare that did its all to mute the
murals on the walls, in which elongated and stylish figures cavorted ceaselessly and without much mirth. What
wasn't painted or chromed or upholstered was wooden.
A large number of different woods from every outpost of
the British Empire vied for the passengers' attention. In-
laid, carved, veneered, solid as in chair and table legs,
worked in ways I can't describe, British wood was the

primary decorative element not just in the grill but all over the ship. It was a nice effect, very comforting. The menu in the verandah grill was as limited as its clientele, which was the point. For those souls to whom caviar was as common as a chicken sandwich and who couldn't have cared less about a supplementary charge, the verandah grill was the place to eat. Winston Churchill always ate in the verandah grill on the *Mary,* that kind of thing. My mother always lunched in the grill and I went downstairs, that kind of thing. I don't know much about dinner in the grill because that was the meal we took together, my mother and I, in the dining saloon. Late at night the grill was something else again. After dinner and after the horseraces and funny-hat contests and bingo games and talent shows in the main lounges, after the movies, after the end of the refined, parlor-type entertainment that had been concocted and announced in the morning's edition of the *Ocean Times,* after decent people went to bed, that's when the verandah grill, like night-blooming cereus, opened its wonderfully iniquitous doors.

The way I looked then mattered. It certainly did to me. I had over the past two years shed twenty rather troublesome pounds at the same time as I let my hair grow long past my shoulders, which I bared on every suitable occasion. Done with cute, possibly even done with pretty, my cheekbones protruded and flared below eyes that were veiled intriguingly with what I now realize must have been perpetual hunger. I was looking the way I wanted to look at last. Move over, Juliette Greco! At eighteen I resembled, if anything, those figures in the murals in the *Mary*'s grill. Excluding the cavorting. I had learned to sit very still and when I sat at a bar like the bar in the verandah grill I did not drink ginger ale and my knees and elbows went the right way. I could even cross one leg twice around the other, which was for me the height of bodily chic, seeing as how thick thighs prevent it. And not just the baby fat but the baby mouth!

With my friend Anya I had practiced and practiced and almost perfected innuendo as a mode of communication. What could be implied was never stated, never denied. I was counting on inscrutability and insinuation to see me through because I was still a little short on experience. Not that I hadn't tried: I just hadn't succeeded. To that end, I had tentative plans for this crossing.

The *Queen Mary* is a little over one thousand feet long. Among other things, she has three funnels, twelve decks, two swimming pools, twenty-four boilers, numerous public rooms and cabins and the regular crew's quarters and storage, service and mechanical spaces. She is held together by over ten million rivets. Four times around the first-class sundeck made a mile of windy walking. I don't know whether to say is or was in all of this because I haven't seen the *Mary* where she's come to grief in California so I don't know what changes have been made in her. Life on the *Mary* wasn't as determinedly festive as on the French Line ships I'd taken before, but to me that year she was just what I wanted: noble and inspiriting, anglo-attractive, especially her officers, who seemed also to be made of fancy British woods, hard and dark. A fair, or perhaps not so fair, amount of the spaces mentioned above were given over to second- and third-class passengers, known on the *Mary* as "Cabin" and "Tourist." It was in that last class that my possibilities traveled in the shape of students, one particularly, whom I had arranged to see. Willy, the older brother of a girl I had just graduated with, a Yale man.

The *Mary* was a tender ship, as I discovered on the second day out when the weather turned for the worse. The purser explained to me that tender is what they call a ship that suffers from vertical instability and therefore rolls more than she should. The *Mary* when I took her hadn't yet had the expensive Denny-Brown stabilizers installed that were, just a few years later, to detenderize her. I went to the Chief Purser to ask for a pass to Tourist. Social mobility was not an advertised feature on board and you needed a pass to move around freely. The purser stalled me with his talk of tender ships. Tender or not, my intentions were strictly horizontal and unless the *Mary* had massive engine failure, a doubtful proposition, time was as short as my nails, which I still bit. Four days across the Atlantic isn't much time at all when you share a cabin with your mother, even a mother who holds court in the verandah grill every midnight and for several hours thereafter. The reason I was pressed for time was that my mother and I were on our way to tour the hill towns of Tuscany and Umbria. This was the first year I went to Europe that I wasn't being shunted off to a Swiss charm school to *perfectionner* my French and my manners. I knew that touring with my mother would hardly be conducive to privacy for either of us. We were booked to fly back from London after a week with my aunt there. I would have only six days at home before I was due to start at Wellesley, a place to which I did not wish to bring even a vestigial memory of maidenhood. I wasn't about to complicate the purser's life with mine, so I really didn't give him the business. The upshot was that I got a pass for a day and the Yalie didn't get one at all. It turned out to be a very minor upshot because we soon found passageways that certain stewards would leave unlocked for certain lively people like us and a good tip.

Willy I knew well although I wasn't sure how well he remembered me. Given my new look, that was probably a plus. Two years earlier, before he left for New Haven, when he was still a senior at Horace Mann, I had a crush on Willy for the six weeks it took to get a cast off his sister Kathy's leg. Kathy and I had been on the 86th Street crosstown bus on our way to the Trans-Lux one afternoon during Christmas vacation to see a rerun of Cocteau's *Orphée*. I accidentally pushed Kathy off the bus as we were getting out, nothing serious. We went into the theater and by the time those two motorcyclists had finished their perplexing ride Kathy was unable to walk. I carried her as best I could to her house, which was two blocks away. We had no money left for a cab. Kathy lived on the third and fourth floors of a converted townhouse with no elevator and dragging her up the stairs was exercise for a month. Once up, we discovered that Kathy's mother was out and irretrievable. Kathy's father was also out of reach because he had died the year before of a heart attack. The first dead father in our class. I remember the exceptional aura that sorrow gave to Kathy, an aura we all coveted although not its circumstance. As the maid was dim, it was I who called the doctor and begged him, just this once, to make a house call. I waited with Kathy, who groaned dramatically for the two hours it took the doctor to get there. By then Willy had come home.

Willy was an entity I hadn't been aware of before, as Kathy was not a particular friend of mine. In the weeks that followed I made sure we became good friends. I visited her almost every afternoon to go over the homework so that she could keep up in spite of her absence from school. What with those stairs and her mother's remorse about having missed some significant moments, it was decided that Kathy should stay at home until the cast was removed. I kept telling Kathy it was just as easy for me to come over as to attempt to do geometry over the telephone. I made time to visit Kathy not only because of Willy but because I wanted out of the mass of instructional arrangements that filled my afternoons. Visiting Kathy provided me with an admirable excuse to drop piano and ballet. Anyway, as I explained to my mother and to Kathy, the fall from the bus was entirely my fault and the least I could do in the way of amends was to visit her.

Willy was the kind of a brother who used to come home from school, knock on his sister's door, look in and ask her how she felt and did she want anything from the kitchen. Hardly the fraternal behavior I was brought up

on. Along with being nice, Willy looked nice, probably
smelled nice too, although I didn't get that close then.
Willy was very tall and had red hair that fell in friendly
little curls down the back of his neck. He also had the
rest of the equipment that was standard in boys of that
year's handsome model. Willy wore a lot of white: white
oxford shirts and whitish pants and a very pale beige
corduroy jacket. Jackets and ties were mandatory at all
the better sort of schools but when Willy came home he
took off his requirements and put on a white tennis
sweater. I had never seen quite so much white on one
boy in January and February. I liked his style, even
though I wasn't sure I was interpreting it correctly. Nice
red-and-white Willy in his room next to Kathy's had to
have overheard us declaiming the stanzas from Keats's
various odes, which we were responsible for memorizing
that month. Into the words "thou still unravish'd bride of
quietness" I put all the intensity I could muster without
bellowing, all the passion I could force. Kathy was doing
the nightingale. Kathy had other problems.

Willy was expecting me. Kathy had told him I'd be on
board, sailing first-class with my mother, and wanted to
invite him to play squash or use the gyms or whatever.
Lady Bountiful was directed by three different stewards
to the Tourist forward lounge, where I found Willy sitting
in a chair that had been bolted to the floor. The stewards
were just putting up roll ropes in that lounge and with
good reason. Willy wasn't feeling very well. With his red
hair and faintly green face, still in whites, Willy looked
like year-old holiday wrapping. Willy wasn't up to chit-
chat but he accepted my invitation to go to the movies
that evening after dinner. In Tourist you got to see movies at difficult times of the day like ten in the morning,
when no one else was scheduled for the theater. The
movie that night was *The Virgin Queen* with Bette
Davis, the title of which I found pretty appropriate. I
explained to Willy about the purser's mean streak and

told him I had already made contact with a corruptible steward. There was a door on C deck, near the Tourist dining room, that would open briefly at a particular moment. If he was there and if he wanted to, Willy could come through it.

By the time the movie ended the sea was calmer, quiet enough to make conversation and drink a viable sport. Imperial Bette had left us both in a sovereign mood and I took Willy up to the verandah grill. My mother was nowhere in sight, probably because my mother is not a good sailor. Willy spoke for a long time about Yale. He told me about things that did not appear in the college catalogues I had been reading all that winter, things like Bones, Mory's, the Lizzie, and Dink Stoverism, preparing me for the J. Press way of life. Willy was planning to major in political science and that's about as far as his plans went. Willy also talked at length about Kathy which, as it was me he was talking to, was natural enough, and about her continuing preoccupation with their dead father, which was not. Willy had a funny speech mannerism that I hadn't heard or hadn't recognized in the few sentences he addressed to Kathy when I used to visit her. He perforated his discourse with long pauses followed by "ehs" pitched one tone higher than the words that had preceded the pauses. It was a mannerism that both emphasized and parodied what he was saying. Until I caught on I kept taking what he said seriously, which wasn't how he meant it. I think Willy was aiming for a sophisticated effect. I think Willy missed. His irony coupled with my innuendo to make a conversation that was barely comprehensible but which gave us both satisfaction of a sort. At two o'clock we called a draw and he walked me to my cabin. We arranged to meet on the sports deck in the morning. He would, he said, take care of the steward.

At sea: uncertainty. The vast and splendid water threatens to deceive us. In the *Mary*'s dining room two tiny crystal ships, two *Queens*, inch together and apart across a painted map of the Atlantic to convince us that our motion has a forward purpose. In a geographical sense we move at sea along lanes laid out long ago in stringent tracks, A through G, on a great-circle route. Summer lanes and winter lanes: to stray from the track is to court disaster, in the form of an iceberg, perhaps. A great-circle route is the safest route, as safe goes. Every time I sailed to Europe I was describing yet another kind of circle, a system more closed than not, over and back and over again. Even though I didn't know it then, my course was as fixed as the *Mary*'s, allowing for a storm or two, all shuttle and spectacle. On an airplane I never felt it but an Atlantic crossing by boat is made for the thinking of long thoughts. As I waited over two hours for Willy to show up the next morning, I had plenty of time for long thoughts, posing like a marine odalisque on a slatted wooden deck chair. Farther down on another deck two men in cloth caps were having a skeet shoot. The white clay discs shone for a second in the sun and then were shattered or dropped down into the sea. Willy arrived at eleven, along with the bouillon, and bent low to give me a kiss much tastier than the soup.

We had a very entertaining day. The games people play on board an ocean liner are diverse and can be strenuous. I took Willy for lunch to our table in the dining saloon. My mother was certainly up on the terrace next to the verandah grill, recovering; she had been asleep when I left the cabin early that morning. After lunch Willy and I took a long constitutional. Tramp, tramp, vamp, vamp: we made some headway. By teatime I was half in love with Willy, as I had to be. Willy, I thought, felt some of the same. Yale had been displaced as a topic of conversation by wider subjects like movies and travel. When you really talk movies you can get across a lot of other things if you want to. After a session in the swimming pool during which Willy kept his hands on my ass and breasts longer than was necessary to support as good a swimmer as I am, he left for his dinner in Tourist, promising to be back that evening.

In the verandah grill on the *Mary* that trip there was a trio that played dance music late at night. The evening before, Willy and I hadn't danced because we couldn't compete with the waves, but that night, the third night out, was a still night. The trio only started around midnight, so until then Willy and I sat in the smoking room just forward of the verandah grill and drank enough brandy to make Monsieur Remy Martin a rich and happy man. My mother had gone to the movies after dinner to see *The Seven-Year Itch,* which both Willy and I had seen, separately of course, twice that winter. That made twenty-eight itchy years, which was enough. When the movie was over, my mother joined us in the smoking room. She was dressed in her usual high-fashion way. On boats, in the evenings, my mother wore long dresses whose drape was calculated to maximize the effect of her passage down the stairs that invariably descended to the first-class dining rooms of luxury liners. For that purpose, soft fabrics and a single color worked best. She, like Willy, wore a lot of white. It must have been a holdover from her many years as a brunette. I myself wore mostly black at night.

I can't say that Willy and my mother hit it off right away. My mother does not appreciate irony, especially irony of a defensive nature. And Willy did not seem responsive to my mother's cunning brand of inquiry, which, if you are not used to it, can be formidable. Naturally I clammed up as soon as my mother sat down. Waves aren't the only thing that rock me. My mother knew Kathy, of course, and had met Willy's mother at one time or another on her rare forays into organized parenthood, but she didn't know Willy. Sweet William was a ripe, collegiate mystery to her, a reddish nut to crack, pick and pop into her mouth. Never mind that I had found the nut. Tough luck on me for not squirreling it away. My mother turned on the charm, a blast of warmth that the captain of the *Titanic* would have found useful for its instant ice-melting properties. Willy's irony evaporated in that heat like cheap perfume, dis-

gustingly. When we went after midnight into the verandah grill, Willy, my mother and I, I was ready to die and
to kill.

I am a believer, generally, but I couldn't believe my
mother that night in the verandah grill when she looked
around and informed us that there was no one whose
company she cared for and that she would join us for one
drink. Willy distinguished himself by whipping out a
chair for my mother with such eagerness, such alacrity,
that he nearly sustained an injury to his ribcage. I did
not believe my mother because it was axiomatic that she
had a friend around. My mother has regiments of chums
lined up on either side of the Atlantic awaiting her arrival. There are relatively few places in the Western
world where my mother does not have a friend or two to
tide her over for a few days. Even in midocean she ac-
crues acquaintances as speedily as possibles appear. My
mother likes a party. She has a terminal case of sociabil-
ity and is not exactly suffering. I've often wondered what
vacuum my mother abhors in herself that makes her,
like that other mother, stuff her life up so. I like a party
too but not a party of three.

The dancing did it. I was outclassed as the *Mary* herself had been by her sister ship: not faster necessarily
but trimmer, steadier, grander. My mother moved before
my eyes in motions so sinuous, so resilient, that they took
the breath away. After a duty dance with me, Willy concentrated on keeping in step with my mother. He was an
extremely smooth dancer for his age. I drank more
brandy than was good for me and threw it up quietly by
the side of the table while Willy and my mother were
doing a samba. A waiter spotted my distress and rushed
over with wet rags. A fuck-up if I ever saw one. I left the
verandah grill in a hurry. My mother and Willy were still
dancing.

I must have passed out cold that night. I have no idea
how long it was before my absence was noticed and dealt
with. I certainly don't remember waking up the way my

mother said I did when she came in to see what she could do for me. I stayed in bed the morning of that fourth day out, my head under the pillow to shut out the light and my mother's face, upon which I did not wish to look. That afternoon we had a little talk in which Willy figured only as a kickoff. In two deck chairs on the sunny side of the ship, our legs wrapped against several sorts of chill, I let my mother have it once and for all. My jealousy spurted out like last night's vomit to dirty us both with the mess I was making of my feeling for her. She wasn't, she said, in any sort of race with me. She said she wasn't.

Superstitions at sea last longer than they need to, perhaps because the dangers are so palpable even now. When someone dies and is buried at sea, the final stitches sewn to close the canvas shroud that covers the body are made through the dead person's nose. Package and content are one, threaded together as the Fates might do it. It makes for a tidy envelope that won't open up as the body slides into the water. It was also, in the days before ships carried doctors as a matter of routine, a way to make sure the corpse was a real corpse. That afternoon after the episode in the verandah grill I buried some innocence at sea. Not the sort I had been planning to bury but another, fresher corpse. I sent one large part of my daughterhood to Davy Jones's locker. The thread I used holds still.

The Captain's Dinner on the fourth night out is a formal occasion and is preceded by choice cocktail parties given by various officers of the ship and by its more ambitious passengers. My mother was invited to four that evening. The party on the *Mary* that no one knows about until you actually get asked to it is the one given by the junior officers. Apart from those short hours, they are not allowed to mingle with the passengers. To the party they give they invite, as a rule, good-looking girls in quite a narrow age range from all three classes. That's what I was told by the informative steward who delivered my invitation. I went. Mourning may become Electra but it doesn't do much for me, my black clothes notwithstanding. I just hoped no one had been around to witness or had heard about my unfortunate behavior of the night before. The party was given in the officers' wardroom on the same level as the verandah grill but farther forward, somewhere under the aft funnel in fact. The rattle in that room was as astonishing as the men were. What I had taken for wood was more like wax, pliable and luminous when lit, a condition which everyone seemed to be achieving rapidly. Not me, not again on that trip. Denys, he spelled his name carefully for Americans, was the junior officer in charge of Navigation and Charts. I asked for and got a mellifluous and intelligible explanation of dead-reckoning and shooting the sun and the stars. It sounded better sport to me than clay pigeons. I had a very nice time, thanks ever so much.

Things cool off on the last day out. The passengers are concerned with their land arrangements, with tips and Boat Trains and cash conversions and packing and goodbyes. Going in the other direction, they think of home and Customs. The crew thinks about the turnaround that will give many of them some time with their families or whatever it is that they cherish on *terra firma*. The con men and professional gamblers who are always aboard make their last and easiest touch in the card room or the verandah grill. Although there is still a busy schedule of games and other events, the air of let's-pretend which energized them is gone on the last day out. The rituals of passage have worked and we've made our way across the big water. Steaming full ahead we wind down fast and the clocks will jump just one more time. My mother and I were debarking early the next morning at Cherbourg, the first port of call for an English liner on its way home.

Part Two

My Continental Divide

VI

I may have broken one heart. That's not much to rave about, in all these years. But the heart I may have broken led in turn to the breaking of some bones and of a mind that was unmendable. Responsibilities. In dreams begin. The poet said so and it must be true, even though I can find nothing dreamy about the way responsibilities finish.

I was in London, passing the second of two collegiate summers spent there on the pretext of working on any old artbook in preparation by the small publishing house owned by my mother's older sister and her children. My uncle, long dead, had left a backlist, a shaky distribution system, and a series of book proposals that took his survivors fifteen years to work through one way or another. Keeping me busy was not a problem. I was sent to the British Museum or to the library at the Courtauld Institute to check caption and bibliographical matter. It was the kind of scut work for which my two years at Wellesley had trained me in a more than adequate manner. It was, actually, about all that my training consisted of. I had learned to shuffle index cards with a skill that dazzled, a brightness that masked whatever thought lay beneath its glow. Between card tricks, in college as in London, I had plenty of time to pursue interests of a less academical nature. Men, for one, and acting, for another. I was hard at work rehearsing a role that might one day move me out of the chorus and into what I took for center stage. In those summers in London the whole city was coaching me. Style, diction, movement: I was a quick study.

My aunt's house, set on a side street off what was known as a "good" square in the center of Belgravia, had on the top floor a tiny flat which happened to be unlet and so was mine for the summer. It was as near as I ever got to my own apartment. The summer before, and in earlier trips more through than to London, I had lived downstairs with my aunt and her youngest daughter, Liesel, to whom I was close in age. Two older cousins, married, parents, were extraterritorial beings. Liesel was in Perugia doing Italian that year, and my aunt said she thought it would be fun for me to be on my own for once. The sort of thing that wouldn't have occurred to her sister my mother.

My aunt lived on the lower three floors of that narrow, white-pillared house in a cocoon of watered silks that were draped at every window and on every sittable surface. A butterfly perpetually on the brink of emergency, my little blonde aunt flittered from room to room and never lit for long in any one place. A few passages of Chopin here, some half-written letters there, open books everywhere. It wasn't until night fell that she settled and, on those evenings I wasn't out, we talked lavishly. My aunt's development had been arrested, her children always said, by the premature death of their father. I disagreed. To me she was full-grown: gorgeous and understandable. We never once, as was my unhappy habit with her sister my mother, shouted at each other. To her children, naturally, she was something else. I could see that.

My aunt had, as did my mother, a deep and faithful commitment to food. Not as eaters, either of them, but as ritualists. The family that eats together stays Jewish. Friday nights in London and New York were command performances. No child, grandchild, transient relative or faintly hungry friend within a reasonable radius could not show up. My aunt, I have to admit, was more aggravating than my mother on this point, but the company was better. In my mother's house widows flocked like sparrows to her table, gray-brown and shrill, wintry. Being a widow herself, my aunt would have few of these unfortunates when she could help it, and preferred to fill her long basement dining room with young people, usually her children's friends, and authors whose works she published. On the second Friday I was there Daniel Pressler, whom I hadn't met before, came for dinner. He was seated next to me and I was unable to shake him for the rest of the summer.

Eligible, near thirty, pale and speckled like some deep-water creature, Danny was encased in a bathyspherical shell of shyness. His large brown eyes peered at me through an aperture that, as it seemed to be made of one-way glass, I couldn't see into. Danny hung on my words. He lit cigarettes, held doors, subsequently brought me chocolates and violets and behaved altogether chivalrously. I was not used to gentlemen callers and his comportment gave me the creeps. Danny's father had been my uncle's friend and banker in Berlin, a silent partner in the publishing venture. He had preceded my uncle to London to set him up there early in 1939, after the events of the *Kristallnacht* made a Jewish business in Germany a high-risk affair. It was an old and still impressive debt, one with which my aunt would not let me trifle. So I had to allow Danny access, even if limited. There wasn't, to be honest, an alternative situation. My previous summer's interest had expired in the chill of winter and long distance.

Danny followed me, appearing like clockwork at noon to hover over any desk at which I found myself. I know

he called the Press each morning to ask where I had been
sent for the day and of course they told him. Danny was
a solicitor and had very recently started his own firm
with money he inherited from his father, who had died
earlier that year. I could tell Danny was neglecting his
work. As mine was highly neglectable I let him squire
me, just so, around the English countryside in his Daim-
ler, not every but many afternoons. I liked that. I liked
the teas by a river's edge, plates and spoons clinking as I
Woolfed down real crumpets and made the conversation,
a kind of fine and dandy blithering about life and my
studies in America, about my hyperurban family in London, for whom the gauzy landscapes we sat in were no
more than the source of the raspberries my aunt bought
by the truckload. Was I taking advantage? It was not
normally my strong point but I was, I must have been. In
dreams begin nightmares.

In the evenings Danny's largesse ran to the theater
tickets for which, as an aspiring if questionable actress,
I had a great thirst. Even Glyndebourne the Impossible
was attained through the skill of Danny's booking agent.
On Friday nights and at least one other night each week,
Danny sat at my aunt's dinner table. He was the quietest
man. Talk washed in pools around him, lapping at him,
scarcely wetting him. His occasional responsive mur-
murs indicated that he had a firm grasp of whatever
topic was being discussed, so I never took his silence for
stupidity. It was so hard to draw Danny into a conversation in any substantial way that I soon stopped trying.
His silence was more of a relief than a challenge. The
crumpets, the plays, my impressions: I could keep a glib
ball rolling.

One night about two weeks before I was to go home, on
our way back from a revolting presentation of *Titus An-
dronicus* that left me gagging, Danny asked if he might
come up to my flat. Once up, he asked, gracefully I
thought, if we might make love, a request I denied as I
should have done the first one. I was grateful, to be sure,

but I couldn't express my gratitude to Danny in any way more physical than the slack and friable kisses we had been exchanging for the last ten days or so. Danny was just too gelatinous for me. I felt if I truly touched him my hand or mouth might sink into his flesh, I might disappear, could drown in his squashiness. And on top of *Titus!* Danny, not mad but limper, left.

My refusal did not seem to have made a difference to Danny and for the rest of my stay we went on as before, he mooning and I sunning a bit too theatrically perhaps. For a going-away present Danny gave me a voluminous shawl that had gold threads running warpwise through blue-and-white chiffon. My aunt called it shot silk. I called it unwearable. Danny told me he planned to come to New York during Christmas, when I would be home, and he hoped I would save a week for him. I would, I said, and why not?

Danny's trip to New York was not a success: not for him and not for me. I was distracted and temporarily destroyed by a crab-carrying Law School sex maniac who had managed to transmit some of his enthusiasm and a good part of his disease to me in the short time since I had met him, scratching away (how *could* I have known) in Boston. I came home to be disinfected, not to run a visitors' bureau, but I had promised Danny a week and I had to give it to him between appointments with my mother's gynecologist. Dr. Bergholz swore eternal secrecy. It was good of him, really, because along with all my other troubles I was stony broke that month and couldn't cross his palm with the requisite silver. I wouldn't, couldn't, believe that he would charge my mother for those visits. The crab, as I now thought of him, was home in Seattle plaguing the entire West Coast from top to bottom, probably bubonically.

My parents, who had known Danny and his now-defunct family for many years, were delighted with Danny's courtship of me. He had a good profession, was handsome enough, rich: all those pragmatic extras on which maidens like myself were meant to focus. During the days, Danny and I went to museums, quick-stepping through centuries in an hour's time. One afternoon I took Danny to a movie at the Modern. It was, I said, a New Yorkish thing to do: not the film as much as the waiting on a line that functioned as a primitive version of a sin- gles' bar. Over the years I put quite a lot of time in on that line. My father loaded us up with opera and theater tickets for the evenings. We lunched. We dined. We shopped. I itched. I loved parts of that week, although I could as easily have been Dannyless. The one sure thing I was learning at Wellesley was that I needed New York or a good facsimile of it. In spite of the high cost of ad- mitting it to myself, I was not very comfortable out there in the heartland, under the dome of spacious skies from which the rain that made me grow did not fall.

After a week, culture-ridden and uninfested, Danny went back to London no farther along a road which, al- though I did not intend to travel it myself, I hadn't the presence of mind to close off completely to him. My par- ents frothed. I could hardly explain to them how the blue-plate-special combination of my pubic problem and Danny's glaucous, fishy flesh had queered the week and him for me. Eschewing marital possibilities, I told them Danny was too old and too quiet. It was a point not at all well taken.

The rest is hearsay and reconstruction, only in part observed by me or anyone else. It so happened that Danny went back to London and into a decline, as it was at first and politely called. His decline consisted of not going to work. He told my aunt, whose concern as a pa- rental pinch hitter extended well beyond daily phone calls, that he was tired, totally exhausted by New York, the flight and a grippe. Except for its duration, it seemed to be a standard English complaint. Danny did not, ap- parently, say much about me although at the time he was writing me letters every other day proposing everything from marriage to marriage. As he had never said anything of the sort to me *viva voce,* I wasn't quite prepared for the rapidity and directness with which these proposals appeared. I refused, of course, more than once, and soon stopped answering his letters, which then stopped arriving.

After three weeks, concern became alarm and so on. My aunt called in a specialist who took a quick look at Danny and called in another. A nervous breakdown, that catch-all condition, was diagnosed and Danny was sent to a clinic in Maidenhead-on-Thames, locale of one of our more genteel tea parties. He escaped immediately. As he was a voluntary patient and hadn't shown signs of being seriously ill, few precautions had been taken with Danny's live-in arrangements. It must have been a snap for him to walk out as he did, fully dressed, on the third night he was there.

Danny made his way to Paddington Station, where he waited for the morning departure of the Cornish Riviera Express. Danny lived for eight days on the trains going back and forth between London and Penzance. He must sometimes have slept in station hotels; the connections aren't all that frequent. I wonder if Danny ever got on the bus that runs from Penzance to Land's End. It took a private detective, the Bank of England and British Railways—a most unlikely trio—more than a week to find Danny. The clinic had alerted my aunt when Danny fled. She was listed as his next of kin, although he had an uncle, his mother's brother, who lived in comparative squalor somewhere in the East End. My aunt definitely didn't want the police brought in, because she thought it would rebound in some way on Danny's professional life, so she hired a private detective to track Danny down. The fellow was, she told me later, as perfectly seedy as any Hammett fan could wish for. After six days of checking hospitals, hotels and local morgues, the man went to Danny's bank. He had finally figured out that money was

something that Danny wasn't used to doing without. Yes,
the B. of E. said, some checks had been cashed but that
was privileged information. My aunt, who has a real flair
for hysteria, was able to convince the branch manager
that this was, although not in official hands, a very ur-
gent matter. It took two days for the detective to perceive
the pattern of Danny's check-cashing and to link it to a
railway schedule. He notified all the station masters
along the route. Oddly, they hadn't even wondered about
their repeat passenger. Within a few hours Danny's position was pinpointed. Along with my aunt and one of my
cousins, who had been at Oxford with Danny, the detective boarded the train at Exeter, unhappily heading in a
westerly direction. They all rode down and back up again
with Danny, whom they escorted to Maidenhead. Danny
was not talking.

Now in a situation of maximal security, Danny did not
respond to the treatments the doctors devised for him nor
did he speak. My aunt visited him regularly. Never a star
mathematician, she put one and one together and wrote
to ask me what had happened in New York. This is
where I came in, for a second time. I honestly didn't
know what had happened in New York. Nothing, I
thought. I told her about the airmail proposals and refus-
als and she told Danny's doctors, who must have reckoned it was at least a line to go on. So they went on it and
I was implicated, not fairly but squarely, smack in the
puddle of Danny's dampest depression. I wanted to ab-
dicate, Edwardly, from those responsibilities begun in
dreams that were not my dreams but I didn't have that
royal flash and force. So when everybody said how essential it was, and when a plane ticket from Boston to London and return appeared in my mailbox just before
Easter vacation—too generous, Daddy—I went where I
shouldn't have gone. I knew it.

Danny before my eyes: a sudden fossil, so pallid. To
others he did not but to me he spoke in whispers, in
words I could not differentiate one from another, a jum-
ble. On a lawn just-green down to the riverside I pushed

the rolling chair he sat in. I did not know why he was so frail, unable to walk. Virginia had the strength one day to march right in and under but Danny wouldn't, I knew, go to a watery grave like that. Water was Danny's element, not a death. I was right. It wasn't watery, or a grave, but ice. I left as soon as I decently could after an interview with Danny's doctors, during which I was just about as speechless as Danny.

In London we all chewed over the facts as we knew them, which was to say hardly at all. Danny's uncle was summoned to dinner on Friday night. He came in wringing his hands, sweating, and promptly had a heart attack on my aunt's best sofa. Which if it wasn't true might be amusing. He was rushed to a hospital and released after two days of observation. At least something went right. We chewed some more. My aunt and my cousins did some heavy remembering. At Oxford, at school earlier, as far back as Berlin they went looking and what they found was little enough but enough to reprieve me. Reasons one, two and three drawn from the magic hat of time past and probably indisputable. Danny's mother, who had died when he was five, was a bit of a *nerveuse* herself when my aunt recalled her, what with all those vapors that required constant medical attention at a variety of Middle-European spas. The Blitz. Terrible for everyone but wasn't it worse, somehow, for Danny alone with his father in a vast and unpleasant house near Hampstead Heath, with only their own cellar, not a proper shelter, to sit in, companionless? And the rigors of law and his father who, when his wife died, determined to devote a life to Danny, his only issue, and did so in spades. That father, dead of cancer less than a year ago, who hadn't told his son of thirty he was sick so as to spare him. My cousin Liesel made a production out of that last one and was very relieved for me. I went back to America with something like a pardon tucked into my pocket. I was nothing more than the straw etc., and my timing was lousy. Cold comfort, very cold.

My visit had an effect. Perhaps not the desired one but

an effect nonetheless. Danny began to talk again. What he spoke was German baby talk. This really let me off the hook, which was exactly what I wanted to be off of. What evasion! Danny's infantilism and my stale urge for exemption were flip sides of such a second-rate record. As there were no doctors in Maidenhead who were proficient in German baby talk, in spite of whatever Freudian training they might have had, Danny was moved, I heard, to a clinic near Hexham, in Northumberland, where there was someone who could listen to him intelligently. Danny's uncle was consulted but not summoned, for obvious reasons. More radical treatments were started: insulin shock, electric shock, lithium, the works. There were no more polite words for Danny's decline. Danny was no longer allowed to have visitors and after a while my aunt stopped referring to him in her infrequent letters. Suddenly I had graduated, spent part of a year in London at the London School of Economics, keeping very clear of my aunt and all mention of Danny, had gone back to New York to work, to marry, to be pregnant, and again, faster and faster. Danny spilled from my mind as silently as he had from his own.

Denouement: the unknotting. Daniel P. with reasons one, two and three escaped to the moors some five years later like Magwitch on the marshes only Pip wasn't there with a pie. I can't believe there were any expectations, not after such a time. This is purest hearsay, filtered through at least two level heads and one not so level. It was three days before they found Danny, curled, cublike, whimpering in a hole beneath the gorse. As it was an unusually severe February, Danny was frozen. Exposure, they call it, although nothing is revealed. Danny lived but he lost both legs, one well above the knee, due to the frostbite. A textbook case. Two legs lost, one mind blown by the wind of unutterable want, a person less: it all adds up. After they found and defrosted Danny, the doctors, as helpless as Danny was harmless, sent him home, where he lives now with a nurse-companion who bakes ginger cookies, always, that I have with my tea when I visit Danny, which is a thing I do every few years when I am in London. Here I come again. What the poet meant was that in the wake of dreams is a slipstream we're sucked into, willy-nilly and greased with guilt, where we glide until we crash land in an unmarked field and maybe somebody walks away from the wreckage and maybe somebody doesn't. Danny still speaks only German but of a grown-up sort now. As that is a language I have strenuously avoided learning, our conversations are as one-sided as ever. Danny peers at me as liquidly as before and I still can't see through his eyes. He has over the years recovered many of his faculties.

VII

You used to hear of something called a "sleep cure." At one time it was, and perhaps is even still, a big business on several Swiss mountainsides. Narcotic and nourishing fluids were dripped through tubes into your arms and you would sleep and sleep and sleep until anxiety was dreamed away. I'm not sure if doctors whispered pertinent suggestions to the dreamers or if just slumber did the trick. Although it must have been done many times for sound fiscal reasons, I can't imagine a sleep cure being prescribed for anything more distressing than the malaise, a sort of motion sickness, which overtook me in my last year at college. Without benefit of expensive medical advice, I too hit upon stasis as a cure-all. And if you don't count the prepaid tuition and board charges, which I didn't, I slept for free.

After three years of conspicuous use of No-Doz, my energies, real and chemical, ran out. I had everything I agitated for in college: the highest marks and prizes and men and starring roles in major theatricals and meaningful relationships with certain younger professors, male and female. What I didn't have was the slightest notion about the tomorrow that was coming fast around a corner. In the sense that education is a preparation, I was not ready. Not engaged emotionally or in any other gear, not interested in graduate school, unacculturated and unreconstructed, unable to make choices long- or short-term, I fell asleep. The will to vacillate works in mysterious ways.

What made my sleep practicable was that in November my roommate upped and married a Hungarian engineering student at M.I.T. whose Slavic nature made it difficult for him to agree to wait until June. As she packed her bags and left, I drowsed off until the middle of January. I used to sleep sixteen or eighteen hours at a stretch, primarily in the daytime. At night I'd wake for a few hours and eat something, write papers, shower, and by five in the morning I'd be asleep again. Once a week I forced myself to stay up until nine A.M. so I could bike to the market in the town of Wellesley and buy groceries for my nocturnal meals. Attendance at classes was not required, and as a senior doing an honors program I had few assignments. Whatever papers had to be done I did. They were handed in for me by the same friend who slipped notes under my door about what was due when. I did not answer mail, phone calls or the housemother's knocks, which sometimes woke me and sometimes didn't. I telephoned my mother early in the morning on my shopping days, before she locked herself into her bathroom for what I now recognize as the long and wet necessaries of older women. I managed to get myself home on a train for Christmas and slept away the vacation, pleading overwork. Asleep, there was no way to discuss what I was going to do next and thereafter.

When you sleep for long periods of time your skin flaps because there is a loss of weight and muscle tone. Hair falls, legs jelly, and eyes when open are clarified. At night I'd look at myself by lamplight in the mirror and see bones I had never seen before in places I hadn't thought were bony. I liked the look of death on the verge, only a rim of slack skin separating now from no more. I toyed with my morbidity, slowly playing out the string of a kite that wasn't flying right. I toyed more privately than others. The year before, in a group of buildings we called The Quad, a girl had died in a closet, bloodied and abandoned by a coven of self-appointed angels of death masquerading as campus abortionists. Morbidity lives like a canker in the heart, foul and pervasive, *le dernier cri.*

Since nobody heard me, I decided to wake up one night when I saw more socket than eyeball and it didn't look so good. Being vain seems to have functional imperatives. It wasn't that easy to move from torpor to action because on the one hand I was addicted to sleep and on the other I still had no rise-and-shine solution for September. Day by day I stayed up later in the mornings, fifteen minutes at a time. It took two weeks to make it down to breakfast in the dining hall. Two weeks after that I could get through my morning classes and lunch. After lunch I napped and then went in to Cambridge to mooch around at the Bick and, later in the day, at the Brattle. I had a lot of friends with cars and someone always drove me back to Wellesley when I lolloped into sleep, usually between ten and eleven at night.

Among my friends I had one in particular whose presence in my life I began to see as a directional signal pointing to some questions I wanted to ask myself. I wasn't yet up to thinking about answers. First things first. I fixed on Walker Wainwright as a kind of final exam I had to pass in order to graduate as an American person of my own. Wasn't that a question, before and after all? Wasn't it? What was I and where did I fit in? Fucking global ambivalence! I had spent so many years teeter-tottering between two cultures and their appropriate modes of behavior, swinging one way, sliding another, that I was like playground equipment. I rusted. I repeated. Another generation would use me. Being in love with Walk could be number one in a series of dots to connect on a line that might lead me beyond the need to sleep again. Of course he more than liked me, we established that quickly enough, which is what made it all possible. In the story, too, he woke her with a kiss.

Porcellian, Pudding, meaty Walker Wainwright. Blond and broad and as aristocratic as is advisable in America, Walk lived in Eliot House and a world as remote from mine as Mars. But one fact was that Walk grew up in West Hartford right next door to Wallace Stevens and anybody who called Stevens Uncle Wallace couldn't be thick. A corollary fact was that Walk was not what he seemed to be. Before he died, Uncle Wallace had worked his tricks through the privet hedges on Westerly Terrace and into the scratch football games, and maybe the smell of oranges wafted through Walk's house too on Sunday mornings, so that by the time Walk got to Harvard he had more than thirteen ways of looking at any old bird. I just happened to be writing my senior thesis on the man.

I had met but not gotten close to Walk in May of the previous year when I played Regan to his Lear. I was never the Cordelia type, not me. Walk's Lear was immature, as it had to be, but so fine that I tabled him for future consideration. At the time, I had two situations more awful than amorous on my hands and I couldn't see initiating a third. When I got the part in *Lear,* an Eliot House Drama Club production, I more or less had to move into Cambridge to keep up with the rehearsals. The only place I could find to stay, I really tried, was in the apartment of a Law School reject of mine, only recently rejected, whose idea of loving attention consisted of occasionally allowing me to change the sheets we were always in the process of dirtying. I swallowed my pride, along with some other things, and begged a bed again. It came with conditions that I met with distaste but promptly. Artists, as they say, make sacrifices. I had also, in London the summer before, unwittingly started something that was finishing in the worst way. Not for me, but for the man in England whose unraveled state was on my mind a lot. So Walk would have to wait. Wait, Walk, wait. See Jane sleep. See Jane wake, Walk, soon.

Awake, then, I settled in with Walk. Not into Eliot House; that was not an available option. In those days before the pill flooded sex, parietal rules were dams that held some of our waters back. What I settled into was the crook of Walk's arm, into the small of his back and the elegant turn of his mind, surprising myself with the intensity of my wish to be gentled by him. Gentling was what Walk did best. As a lover, he lacked a certain singleness of purpose. Cosiness substituted for foreplay. Like saccharin, it's not a wholly acceptable substitute. Where opportunities did not exist we were able to invent them with the help of Walk's car, absolutely a *deus* of a *machina* if I ever saw one. Walk drove an old runabout that his father had treated the way no gentleman should treat a car. Not that we used the car for anything as dim as vehicular passions, but it took us to cheap motels in a ring around Boston. Natick, Framingham, Dedham, Brookline, I finally got to know the countryside. The motel business was new to me because every man I had been involved with on an overnight basis during my college career had been a graduate student in his own apartment. It wasn't that I was spoiled, not in the slightest, it was just that I wasn't used to the suitcase game. It made me edgy, which wasn't a way to be with someone who lacked, as I've said, and so forth. In the suitcase we packed cartons of orange juice and cellophane-wrapped crumb cakes for breakfast or whatever meal we would make. We also packed books to load down the case in the event that some frisky motelkeeper might want to lift it for us. Sometimes we read the books. I wore a ring that Walk had bought for me in a store on Mass. Ave. Two silver knots joined in what was almost an infinity sign. At the motels, I turned the knots inward so only the band would show.

Several weekends we drove down to Cape Cod and I felt legitimate because there were clothes in the suitcase. Even in winter the Cape smells of tar and pine as soon as you cross the bridge at Buzzard's Bay and turn onto Route 6. It's a smell of warmth and blunt promise, or at least that's how I chose to smell it. I had spent a summer in a camp on the Cape and we went to Brewster to look at the shuttered and scaling cabins that were smaller than I remembered them. Once we drove to Maine for three days. We broke into the house owned by Walk's parents on Prout's Neck and we laid low in every sense so that the caretaker driving by might not see us moving across the large window that framed a view of the sea. That window, Walk explained, was left unboarded, at some risk, so that the Wainwrights could at any time they wanted drive up for a weekend of winter seascapes. Talk about edgy! The house was called a cottage, a word I later learned to read as a euphemism for shabby. An air of calcified gentility hung in the empty rooms, scenting the blue chintz roses and the arrangements of shells and dried grasses in old bottles and baskets. As decoration goes, I liked it. In Walk's room, where we lived, his boyhood collection of local moths and butterflies was pinned onto cardboard squares taped to the wall he could see best when lying in bed. In the center of that wall was a window and it looked like those pale and flaky butterflies had flown in for a visit that lasted too long.

One of Walk's aunts lived in Boston and had inherited, along with a house on Beacon Hill and her hats, a season pass to the Copley Plaza for the Waltz Nights that served as a clearinghouse for that city's quality goods. She invited us to accompany her one evening. I had a little trouble scrounging up the eighteen-button kid gloves that I knew were de rigueur but the dress was no problem. I borrowed my ex-roommate's wedding dress, removed the detachable train, wrapped a red sash twice around my waist, and topped the whole number off with a black velvet vest that was part of another dress I had.

I looked vaguely Spanish, quite effective I thought and so did Walk. Walk in white tie, his own, was superb, a luminous princeling I had to keep touching to make sure he was real and mine. We went to Aunt Emily's for dinner first. There were no other guests. She served us the whitest food: a cream soup and poached chicken breasts and a custard that I was glad to see had at least a crust of brown on it. I think Walk's uncle was having trouble with his teeth. Perhaps that explains the nursery food and why I had such difficulty understanding what he said, which wasn't much. I suppose someone, Walk's mother maybe, had instructed Aunt Emily to check me out and I guess I passed all right. Later, waltzing, we lost them. Walk danced as I did, with more spirit than grace, more feeling than form. Our bodies moved together and apart like parentheses, counterpoised and containing, making love of a sort we hadn't made before. "Goodnight, Ladies" came too soon.

I went home for the Easter break. Walk was going to come to New York for two days and stay with his grandmother at River House, a building on whose doorstep I had set neither foot nor my sights. Walk wanted to meet my parents and then drive me up to Hartford, the weekend before school started, to meet his. Plan A was fully operational: I was at dot number two and loving it. It seemed a decent enough plan to me, although I wasn't quite sure what, apart from me, was in it for Walk. Walk wanted to be an actor and was getting a wholesale supply, a gross, of encouragement from his father. The good-neighbor effect again. Walk had applied to the Royal Academy of Dramatic Art and been accepted for the following term. I wondered if I could manage a year in London without some matrimonial certification to back me up. I had no wish, any longer, to train as an actress. To train, in fact, as anything. Besides, even with a private income to take the heat off, the last thing a young actor needs is a little woman around the house complaining that rehearsals go so late every night.

The second I stepped through the door of my parents' apartment the shouting began. It took me only five minutes to discover how the carefully orchestrated announcement I had been planning to leak slowly had been scooped. Walk was fairly well-known in Cambridge and we hadn't been exactly invisible. I had a cousin at the Business School who was taking an advanced degree in dirty pool. He had a mother with a mouth wider than the Mississippi's. So it goes.

What my father said meant most and I believed him, about sitting *shivah* for me. On low stools, your clothes ripped and the mirrors covered, you sat *shivah* for dead people, not for live Wellesley girls. Dead people you don't see again or talk to or leave money to. Dead people you don't toy with and they aren't pretty by lamplight. My mother yelled about things like being called "filthy Jew" when the dishwasher broke down or you spent too much money or had a fight about anything at all. She yelled about children and Hitler and country clubs and Auschwitz and historical realities. Even though my mother had what amounted to the East Coast franchise on guilt manipulation, what she yelled about were things I thought I could learn to deal with. But after my father spoke, waiting his turn, I didn't know if I could deal with dead. Really dead, maybe, but not dead and alive at the same time to different people. When I finally got out of the front hall where all of this was taking place, so quickly was it sprung on me, I went into my room and called Walk to get him to cancel his leg of the trip for reasons which I couldn't quite give him. My parents, I said, were not feeling well. I heard someone pick up the extension phone in my brother's room.

The Jewish Question: perennial table topic and argument starter, the unclear source of a river of tears. At times it had geopolitical connotations, or religious and dietary overtones, or sometimes even philosophical implications and, occasionally, all of the above. In my parents' house on that day, it referred to intermarriage and the answer was no. What was the matter with me?

Hadn't I been listening all those years and believing what I heard? Or was it that nothing had ever been spelled out for me so emphatically, so unequivocally? I know the *shivah* part was news to me. Until the possibility of Walk appeared, not even a sure thing yet, I had no indication of the terrible form my parents' opposition would take. Perhaps they had never unleashed the *Sturm und Drang* of it because they never believed a daughter of theirs could etc. Or perhaps they had simply forgotten to tell me that, as they had never wanted America in the first place, they had deep-sixed assimilation on the boat coming over: for themselves, for me, for mine.

I'm spiky, an infighter, and I wasn't about to give up. Three days of clogged silence ensued (they had said their piece) and on the fourth I left for Hartford. On my desk where I knew it would be found I left a New Haven Railroad schedule with bright red arrows pointing you-know-where. I even left a telephone number. For openers, I was expected, a condition which generally gets me moving from one place to another. Walk had told me on the phone that his parents were giving a big double-duty cocktail party. It was his sister's sixteenth birthday and this was to be a practice session for her coming out the following year. It was also, he said, a way for me to meet their friends.

The Wainwrights' house was not like their cottage. Set squarely in a large expanse of what would surely be lawn in a month or so, the house imposed. Inside, it was heavy with leather and dull rugs and wood paneling and brasses that could have used a bit of polishing up. Nothing in that chinkless house floated like the space in Prout's Neck, nothing whistled. I arrived late on the evening before the party, and supper had been kept for Walk and me in the kitchen. The Wainwrights were out. Walk's sister was hysterical in what I could see was her own mild and attractive way. Her name was Lorillard, a family name, and they called her Lori. Walk showed me around the house and what I liked best were the books in almost every room downstairs. Not just your Book-of-the-Month-Club specials: real books, shelves and shelves of them in each room, adding measurably to the heavy look. As I rubbernecked the books to get some clues about the people who had purchased them, I had to admit that, titlewise, it wasn't much like home. I said I was tired and went up to bed before the Wainwrights got back. I locked myself in and Walk out, just in case.

Saturday morning it was raining softly when I woke up. Someone—it turned out to be Lori with a breakfast tray—was knocking on my door. Lori said her mother was gardening and wondered if, when I was ready, I would like to join her. Walk was still asleep, Lori said, he always slept late at home. I ate, dressed, and went into the garden for a show of myself and my horticultural ignorance. Luckily it was April and I knew what forsythia looked like. Mrs. Wainwright, kneeling in the mud of a flower-bed-to-be, stood up and started to shake my hand without remembering to take off her mucky glove. She must have had second thoughts because, then, she kissed me, which was better. Mrs. Wainwright had white hair rolled in a pageboy under her Harris tweed hat, and a strong face. By strong I mean angular, somewhat gritty. Lori had given me a pair of gardening gloves and Mrs. Wainwright and I raked and prodded for an hour, tossing stones in a pail, talking of Walk and of acting as a career and Uncle Wallace and Wellesley, where she had gone, she said, a hundred years ago. It was the kind of click-clack you can make mechanically even in difficult circumstances and it left me free to think about why there was a bottle of gin and a glass in the wicker basket Mrs. Wainwright carried her tools in. Ten-thirty in the morning. Rain. Last year's weeds. Those interminable stones. Me. It must have called for a drink or two, although I didn't see her take one.

Mr. Wainwright came home for lunch. On Saturday mornings he golfed. Mr. Wainwright was handsome,

wiry in shape and manner, not wide and accommodating
the way Walk was. He and Walk and I had our lunch on
trays in the library. Mrs. Wainwright and Lori had gone
to the hairdresser, an invitation I declined. I began to
wonder who was preparing for the party. Besides the
Model-T housekeeper in the kitchen, whose legs seemed
to bother her, I hadn't seen any other help. In my
mother's house a party was preceded by a two-day frenzy
of cooking and deliveries and the banshee whirring of
floor polishers. Mr. Wainwright, as if reading my mind,
told me that the bartender and his staff would arrive
later. Mr. Wainwright I could have done without.

I shook a lot of hands that night and smiled a lot of
smiles. With enough of the proper credentials you can
get through anything. Lori and Walk had each invited a
group of friends and we all, we young and younger ones,
found ourselves massing at one end of the big living
room, nattering, making nippy small talk of a scholastic
variety. After everyone else was gone the five of us sat
and ate leftover cheese straws and olives. I was learning:
cocktails meant just that. If I was hungry, Mrs. Wainwright said, there was sandwich stuff in the kitchen.
Mrs. Wainwright said it had been a great success. People
had remarked. Mrs. Wainwright was drunk and Mr.
Wainwright was drunk and Walk was drunk and I was
extremely dismayed. I had seen plenty of drunks at Harvard, Walk included, but they were loud and cheerful
and tended to vomit before they got dangerous. What I
hadn't seen before were polite drunks, people who sat
neatly in their chairs and kept their mouths moving in a
sad and defective approximation of human dialogue.
From a distance, across the room say, you might not
have known. Up close, it was unmistakable and so
smooth an act that I could tell they had been rehearsing
it for a very long time. I began to think that if what is
said is true, that people become their parents, I could be
in real trouble.

The following morning Mrs. Wainwright and I had a

heart-to-heart in her sitting room. Those were her words. It appeared that Walk had already told his parents, some weeks before, that he was more than a bit serious about me. A gun-jumper, that one. Mrs. Wainwright wanted me to know that she and Mr. W. were delighted. She wanted to be sure that I also knew, if Walk hadn't told me, that she had a half-Jewish grandmother on her mother's side. I didn't know if that hot tip was supposed to impress or to comfort me. Walk and I left soon after and I mostly kept my mouth shut on the drive up. I did not mention my parents' intentions. I did not repeat his mother's words to me. I had some sorting out to do, a shakedown.

I once took a course in geology. Science was required then. Schist, magma, drifts and thrust faults, shield areas and the regime of streams: the vocabulary was terrific but I wasn't wild about the rocks. We often went into the field, as the teacher called it, scratching in the ground right behind the old Norumbega Hall, where the course was given. Back from New York and Hartford, away from the threats and the booze, two kinds of tight, that vocabulary surfaced again and I saw that I had come to a continental divide, a high ridge from which I could run off another way. West, maybe west. Dots on a line. The next number was on the horizon and up for grabs. If I connected with Walk, part of me was dead. If I didn't, another part would perish. Which mattered more? That was the question I'd forced, a question that resonated from peak to valley and back again.

In May, in the middle of Generals and final papers and preparations for hoop-rolls and goodbye, Walk began to push me, a thing I dislike. Wake up, Jane, wake up now, dammit! He wanted to marry me and take me to London legally. Although I wasn't really ready to do so, I had to explain the rites of *shivah* to Walk and how they would apply to me. Whereupon he sincerely offered his parents as surrogates. It wasn't quite what I had in mind. Again,

I had started something that wasn't finishing right. Not unwittingly, however, and I loved the man. But when people push me I feel I want to push back. A year had passed since I played Regan to his Lear and my treason was in bloom again. I should have been straightforward, plain-spoken and plain-dealing, an artless girl. Instead I was more cunning than constant, a side-stepper still, bobbing and lurching, a dangler, a fool. I decided to go to London and not to marry Walk. I'd manage it.

VIII

Married men were the mystery meat of my generation in the years before divorce reached pandemic proportions. It came disguised in many sauces, some distinctly spicy. For those of us who managed to complete our education without benefit or prospect of wedlock, that meat was as challenging as it was available. You had to try it once, at least, roll it around in your mouth, chew it up, swallow and wait to see what it could do for and to you. Digestible, yes? If you were hungry enough you ate it without complaint, a steady and often discouraging diet. If you weren't so hungry, you could pass it up the second time. If mildly famished, as I was when I came back from a year in London that had turned out to be disappointingly cloistral, you might want to give that meat a really good try, maybe demystify it if the price was right.

The first part of the scenario went like this. College grad., recent refs., languages, post-nubile, rides subway every morning to work in Greenwich Village, plum of a job, quality lit. mag., lowest wages ever. Two stops downtown enters, daily, fellow straphanger with black curls, gypsy eyes and a midtown destination. When push comes to shove one day early in June they meet. She's maneuvered right, or he has. Mutual underground admiration society forms. He knows a friend of a friend, lucky break. Not quite thirty, snappy dresser, highly paid copywriter for BBD&O with novelistic intentions, eminently handsome. Three days later she's fucking him on West 75th Street, proof again that litero-sexual relations move fast.

On my way uptown every night I'd detour at Sam's house. Even though I was living at home and under a species of parental supervision, I'd made it a condition of my being there that I didn't necessarily have to account for my time. I had a pact with my father that guaranteed my mother's nonaggression. Like all such pacts it was full of loopholes but, by and large, satisfactional. To get to Sam I'd go up two flights of stairs and into the Garden of Eden as plantable in a brownstone floor-through with its best light north. At the window an upwardly mobile jungle of *ficus benjamina,* avocado, schefflera, assorted exotics, succulents and cacti gasped and swished when we left the window open to cool the bed. All that greenery prebreathed my air when I came up for it, perhaps once every hour I was there. By far the lushest plant was the one we lay on, a wide sward of bright lawn, green and thirsty. That lawn was bordered all around by something like a hedge, Sam's marriage, but it was a couple of weeks before I bumped into that hedge. For one thing, my powers of observation were greatly diminished by the happy fact that my eyes were shut most of the time. For another, I am not a snooper and had no reason to open a closet. I did spend a fair amount of time in the bathroom but found no female evidence in there, perhaps because I wasn't looking for it.

Samuel H. for Henry Stern, product of Great Neck High, Dartmouth and his imagination, doing what he wanted to do, words on paper, although it wasn't exactly the syntax he had in mind for himself. Sam's father was a very successful cloak-and-suiter who had taken a big position in New York real estate in the late forties, as quite a few of those men did, their pockets crammed with cash payment for military clothing contracts. Sam's mother was a mover and shaker in Hadassah, North Shore branch. There was one other child, Sam's older brother, who had vanished into one of his father's holding corporations and who would one day emerge to manage more than he could handle. I never met any of these people, I just heard about them one night after the confession barrier had been broken. Prior to that, what there had been of our talk was topical, more topographical. Sam told me that he grew up in a house built like a tank: turreted, solid, unyielding. Around the house were gardens leading down to a patch of beach on the Sound. There was a small sail dinghy moored a few yards out which belonged to the neighbor on the right but which Sam had permission to take out in the cove on which these houses fronted. The sail was gaff-rigged, sometimes tricky. Sam seemed to think that was an important point, judging from the length of time he spent telling me about it.

Sambo became a gypsy one summer on a trip to Mexico with his college roommate when the sun struck him for the first time: the clarity, the load of it in every inlet of the body which opens to receive it. It was nothing like the sun at Camp Takajo in Naples, Maine, where Sam passed fourteen summers in various stages of camper- and counselorhood. Sam said the sun in Mexico made him realize that five senses could do the work of twenty-five if they wanted to, just as heavy water has that tiny edge over the regular stuff. I had been in Italy, so I thought I knew what he was talking about. To be sure, he showed me. I was not a slow learner and the lessons stuck. When I think sexy, I still think gypsy, Mediterranean. Dark, winged thoughts. Two bodies glisten together, glued together, come apart with a loud suck of

sweat and oils. Understand that gypsy is my shorthand
for pleasure.

The way I knew Sam was married was that his best
friend Ronnie the Shrink came to dinner one night and
slipped up, as psychiatrists have a way of doing in the
company of nonpatients. There were no denials served
with the scaloppine. Sam was an outstanding cook. I
learned a great deal from Sam. Sam cooked and I did the
shopping from a list he made for me the night before.
Sometimes I shopped at the Italian grocery stores in the
Village during my lunch break, but if you've ever taken
a rush-hour subway in June with Gorgonzola in your
arms, you'll know why I liked the King Kong market
around the corner from Sam's. And I couldn't resist buying bananas at the King Kong, just a few each time. We
ate in every night, picnicked on the lawn a lot, because
we didn't particularly want to get dressed and go out.
Until Ronnie goofed I didn't know I was supposed to be
invisible. I don't know why Sam invited him; it wasn't
my idea.

When Ronnie left, wagging his tail behind him, Sam
explained that his wife was in the Pacific photographing
volcanic rock formations, in Hawaii that week, on as-
signment for *National Geographic*. She would be away
for at least another month, maybe longer. She was with
a team of geologists and naturalists and he wasn't sure
which other islands they would visit. Open your eyes,
sweetie, and look around. See those photographs hung
on every wall, unframed but matted or mounted, those
murky studies in texture that looked like high-school
darkroom outtakes? See the flowers on one side of the
asbestos gloves in the kitchen? Open the door and see
the two pairs of skis in the hall closet, one long and one
shorter? I got the picture although there wasn't much to
look at because Sam's wife was an exceptionally well-
organized woman who traveled heavy. What she hadn't
taken with her she had put away for summer storage in

boxes on the top shelves of several closets. The bathroom she had stripped clean of personal effects, probably figuring that there wasn't a big supply of quality cosmetics in Rarotonga. The style of the apartment was Early Unisex which, as it didn't run to chintzes, was no tip-off. The plants? Perhaps. Sam was not really a plant person, not a tender of the inedible. Sam told me his wife had fiddled this job for herself because she wanted to travel as much as she could before they had children, which was to be soonest, although there was no pregnancy yet. They had been married five years. There was, he said, a tiny sperm-count problem. I was only slightly relieved to hear it. Sambo, the gypsy man, was a very sweet talker. Within an hour I was on my back again, feeling among other things sorry for him. As there were no children involved, I did not consider that I was poaching.

The wife turned out to be impedimental, no doubt about it. She clotted me, interfering like an embolism with the circulation of blood to my nerve-endings. In the weeks that followed I couldn't feel Sam as acutely as I had before. I would start to run across our lawn and be brought up sharply, a hedge-shy hunter who wouldn't take the jump without a little showboating on the side. One night an electric storm sent a message. The lightning flared and back-lit a large ginkgo tree growing in the garden beyond Sam's window. I saw that I wanted to take the idea of wife, so neatly disposed of, so far-flung by Sam and the *National Geo.,* and bury it in the thick trunk of the ginkgo tree. Certain tribes practice tree burial, I read about it once in that magazine—the Naga, the Andamanese, the Kwakiutl, the Blackfoot and some others. It may be an honest way to go: straight, up. I wished her nothing but the best. The ginkgo tree had blunt, bispatulate leaves, not fingers but lobes. If I buried the idea of wife in the ginkgo tree, those leaves could not reach out to touch me or Sam, with whom I did not share my thoughts on these matters.

On July Fourth weekend we went to Amagansett. Ronnie lent us a house he had rented for the season but couldn't use that weekend because he had a cousin in Detroit who didn't know any better than to get married on a national holiday in the heat of summer. Amagansett in those days was a primitive and sparsely populated annex to East Hampton, a little like the servants' quarters on a large estate. You slept there but you didn't work there. If you were in the life, what you worked was Main Beach in East Hampton, the only beach where you could park a car and make time. On Main Beach you worked the right side or the left side, facing the sea and taking as a center point the narrow strip of wooden decking that led over the hot sand in a line from the bathhouse to the water. The improbably talented and hungry worked both sides of Main Beach. On the right side sat the artists, the sun worshipers, and what passed for the intelligentsia. You rarely saw an umbrella on the right side. On the left side sat families with small children and large ambitions, the women often in neat, skirted bathing suits and the men lugging hampers stocked with Kool-Aid, peaches and moist washcloths. Umbrellas abounded on this side and were generally festooned with tiny bathing suits hung from the spokes to dry before they were put on again for the sole purpose of getting wet. The conversation on the left side was inordinately concerned with parties, replays and preplays. Far beyond the families to the left sat the homosexuals, whose beach habits I did not examine as thoroughly as I might have. Now, I believe, all of that has changed and the boundaries have been redrawn, perhaps more fairly. I knew all about Main Beach because my parents had for a couple of summers sacrificed Switzerland and Venice on the altar of suitable settings from which to launch their marriageable offspring, of whom I was only one. So far with no results. A gondola would surely have worked out better. My parents were, actually, in residence in East Hampton that weekend. They thought I was in Lenox for the Beethoven weekend at Tanglewood.

Ronnie's rental was just what you might expect from a man of limited funds and absolutely no tact or sense of privacy. It was a cabinlike structure of two main rooms whose functions were barely differentiated as each one of them contained a bed. The room with a lamp in it we used as a living room. In the back a lean-to housed the kitchen and the bathroom. If Mies van der Rohe had spent twenty-four consecutive hours in a house like this one, he might have had important second thoughts about less and more. The house was placed on the top of a dune within sound but not sight of the sea, which was fine. What wasn't so fine was that the only other house in sight was set so close to Ronnie's that they seemed to have one wall in common. You couldn't get any closer and still be in a separate accommodation. And what was worse was that the house next door, on that weekend, was inhabited by a mob of off-duty customers' men who turned into maniacs in their spare time. They had obviously cornered the flesh market on eastern Long Island that weekend because a steady and swollen river of cars driven by females or impersonators rushed right by our window on the driveway we shared with the other house. There were never less than eight cars parked in a semicircle around the minuscule porch of that house which was a twin to ours. Not only did we get up-to-the-minute reports on the Exchange's activity of the week before, we heard every shrill and croak of every conceivable orgasm in a wide variety of combinations. Twos, threes, fives, mores: that group could have used a few extra sexes to play out their repertoire.

The reason we heard and saw so much was that we were housebound. It rained all weekend and Sam's car was on the fritz, having broken down on the trip out. We couldn't have worked Main Beach if we'd wanted to, which after two days next to that unlovely house began to look like a preferred alternative in spite of the rain and my invisibility factor. Sam drove a Jaguar XKE at a time when the penetralia of foreign cars were still largely a matter of conjecture on American roads. A garage in Bridgehampton was trying to locate a length of rubber tubing of an arcane bore-size, without which the radiator leaked uncontrollably. Sam didn't like the uncontrollable, even if all it meant was stopping for water every five miles. The tubing was promised for Sunday and the car sat tight in Bridgehampton. A mechanic had delivered us and some groceries we had stopped for to the house, swearing he'd be back with the Jag by noon on Sunday. Predictably, no one had a car to rent us on that busy weekend. Unless I called my parents and borrowed a car from them we were stuck with the rain, the noxious one-way traffic next door, and Ronnie's generous mistake.

Sam was in the dumps that weekend and so was I. What should have, could have, been three days of *luxe, calme et volupté* wasn't. Things were slipping and oozing like the dunes in the rain. First the car, then the neighborhood, the weather. To further complicate matters, I was oozing too, having gotten my period on the drive out. I was a big bleeder then, very irregular. I hadn't bled before with Sam. Sam said the blood on the insides of my thighs and on the sheets didn't bother him but it sure deterred me. I was so womanish, too sappy and open to feel a necessary friction. In all dictionaries including the multi-volume OED the word that comes after woman and its derivatives is womb; as if that were another way to say us, as if no real separation can occur and maybe it can't. I wanted not to bleed for Sam, to have him fill my womb and staunch, for a while, the periodic tables of a chemistry I wasn't crazy about. All of a sudden I wanted Sambo's baby, a thing he wouldn't and probably couldn't give to me. I began to realize that there might be more to this business than the pleasure we shared, that I was pretty far gone in fact. I seeped and clotted some more and Sam's wife was there and she wasn't.

It was still raining on Sunday when the car arrived, in time for us to get a reasonable head start on the traffic back to New York. Sam's habitual good humor returned in direct ratio to the miles we covered. By the time we got to the Smithtown bypass off Route 25, I felt I could ask a significant question, one that had to do with a foreseeable future. That was my first error. I only made two, the second of which was in my expectations about Sam's answer. I phrased my question as delicately as I could but, still, I think I blew it. On the other hand it needed some blowing after that bloody weekend and my uterine fancies. I asked Sam if he didn't think some classification might be in order: mine, his, hers. We were like three monogrammed towels heaped together in a corner in the bathroom, not clean, and not dirty either, more damp than usable. Sam didn't see it that way. Sam said he had as little reason to leave his wife as he had to give me up. He wanted to get another apartment, just a room really, that we could use ad lib. What would be even better, Sam said, would be for me to move out of my parents' house and take a place of my own. I considered it for thirty seconds. Sam was spoiled. Like many second and last children, Sam was intact, intractable. He looked and was a man who called the shots. Sam wasn't rigid, he was just always right: a perfect phallocratic specimen. Sam had no residual twinges about his life so far, no should-have-beens or might-have-dones vibrated on the autoharp in his head. There was nothing correctible, he thought, that time would not take care of. His infertility, for example. The book and a child would come in due course. Green grow the rushes, O. Rush the green-growers and green won't grow. The seed case puffs and scatters in the wind of haste. Ripeness is all, is all, is all, sings a finch in the tree. I had two weeks left in which to create a dependency that would be as natural as birdsong in C major. It was superlative sex, impedimenta and all, and it had to continue to blooooom, yes.

When we got back to 75th Street Sam's wife was there,

having come home early because she had picked up a case of dengue fever that she preferred to sweat out in her own bed and not in Papeete. She wasn't the sort of person who, sick or not, dumped suitcases in the hall when she came back from a trip. As she was asleep and the lights were off, we woke her when we turned them on in the bedroom. She was a very pretty woman. Sam introduced me as Ronnie's cousin from Detroit. That did it. It was an easy finish to something that had already ended fifty miles back on the bypass.

IX

The Cathedral of Notre-Dame in Strasbourg is made, as
are many buildings in Alsace, of a soft red stone that is
perpetually in a state of decay. Driblets of rock trickle
down the flanks of the cathedral after a bad storm in
winter and there are cracks like corduroy that mingle
and blend with the carving for which Notre-Dame is
known. On the street that runs behind the cathedral
there is another red structure with big white-rimmed
windows marching evenly across the front of it. This
building is catercorner to the cathedral on the street
which they share and you can see, from a certain angle
when the light is good, patches of the rear of the church
reflected and distorted in the large windowpanes. The
man who made the photograph got it almost right. For
his picture, he posed the eighteen children of that year's
third-grade class in front of the door, also outlined in
white, of that school which sits behind Notre-Dame. It is
a large-plate photograph and I can examine details like
fissures in the wall and ribbons braided into the lower

part of the pigtails that many of the girls wear, but I can't quite make out the reflections. All the boys kneel on one knee in the front row with their hands stuck, clearly on command, into the pockets of their short pants. The girls stand behind the row of boys. Judging from the children's clothes the weather must be warm but the teacher, seated in the center, wears a fur piece. An animal's head with its mouth gripping its own tail forms a circle that rests on the teacher's shoulders. Tiny feet dangle. The teacher wears a hat with a brim that slopes down but does not cover her eyes, which I can see are crossed. As four of the eight boys in the photograph have crossed eyes, I suspect mockery more than a local epidemic of strabismus. The year, written in white ink in the lower left-hand corner, is 1939. Of the eighteen children in the picture there were four who were Jewish. Of the four Jews there is one alive, the third boy from the right, one of those with his eyes crossed, who grew up to be a man I married. A my name is Alice and my husband's name is André. We live in America and we sell Apples.

Seven photographs and a postcard: images as sharp as knives to slice up a bit of a past with. Mint, no foxing, unrippled, an occasional tear in a corner, it may be more than most have. André's mother did give me a few other snaps, all that she had, but these will do. They are for me actual events I can think about. I can not think about, say, a gas called Zyklon B or about blame, either personal or collective. Not a lack but a surfeit of feeling is what chokes back the voice, the thoughts, deep down in the gut below the heart, indelibly. I can not think about what is in the eyes and ribs we see in some photographs or about what is in some others that we do not see. I can not.

B her name was Berthe, the concierge of the villa in Dinard where André was spending the holidays with

his mother in the summer after the class picture was
made. As it was new, André carried the picture with
him to Dinard. Living in the villa with André and his
mother was Oncle Philippe, his mother's younger
brother, on vacation from his studies at the Sorbonne. It
was Oncle Philippe who showed André the octopus routine. Dinard, on the coast of Brittany, has like many
Channel and North Sea beaches a great range of tide. At
low tide boys seem to like to wander on the flats and fish
for the octopi that live tucked under the large boulders
on the sand whose bottoms are exposed when the water
recedes. With a thin metal pole that has a crook in one
end of it, the boys tap the underside of the rock and listen
for the plink of metal on stone. When they don't hear any
noise is when they've hit an octopus, which they then
hook with a twist of the pole and pull in. As André
would not eat these animals, he gave them to Berthe who
did. The snapshot shows André with a wicker basket in
one hand and the pole over his other shoulder. Tiny arms
hang over the basket's rim. André's mother, Mme.
Dreyfus, stands to one side of him, not the octopus side.
She is wearing slacks, very modern, so crisp and white
that they glisten still on the coated paper. The concierge,
on André's other side, is having a grand time posing for
her husband, who was pressed into duty as photographer
because Oncle Philippe was sleeping late that morning.
The three stand together on a sun-struck terrace in front
of the house, which is only partially blotted out by one
finger that Berthe's husband neglected to remove from a
corner of the lens of M. Dreyfus's rather overwhelming
camera. André says that Berthe used to put the octopi's
tentacles over the granite edge of the sidewalk and then
beat those arms with cobblestones to soften the flesh and
make it edible. André fished just about every day and
kept a tally of his catch so that when his father arrived
on weekends he would have some interesting figures to
throw at him. André's father, whom I never met, came
frequently in July but at the beginning of August was

remobilized into the army he had served in with some
distinction in earlier years. His father, André says,
spent most of August in a bunker on the Maginot Line
near Haguenau in preparation for what was going to be
a very funny war.

The likeness of a man I never met, a marked man.
Starting at the bottom then: boots glossy with wax
rubbed hard, the trousers creased just so, tunic belted
and in the left lapel a tiny speck of a rosette that I might
not see if I didn't know to look for it, broad across the
shoulders, he wears glasses and is bareheaded. M. Dreyfus posed in uniform for André, who was still trying to
figure out the niceties of his first camera, a Brownie box
model that he had been given for his eleventh birthday,
in October. Legs apart in a stance of utter and obviously
habitual confidence, his hands clasped behind his back,
M. Dreyfus thrusts his decorated chest at the world beyond André's simple apparatus. André has planted his
father beside a thick and furrowed tree, a kind of locust
I believe, that André says was in the garden of the villa
in Fontainebleau next to the toolshed, a tree he never
saw in leaf because they only spent a winter there.
André and his mother hadn't gone back to Strasbourg
after the summer because home was out-of-bounds
being, as it suddenly was in September, a war zone. They
were in Fontainebleau because it was central, reachable
on a weekend pass from whichever Front might develop.
Oncle Philippe came down often from Paris, sometimes
bringing André's grandmother with him, although she
did not like to move around too much since the death of
her husband three years earlier. By the time of André's
birthday they were settled in and André was doing all
right in his new school although, he says, he missed his
pals. The camera was a present from Oncle Philippe and
Grand-maman Claire and André says the roll he shot of
them all that day fell from his hands and unwound as he
was unloading the camera, unfortunately. In André's

photograph of his father, made later and already showing a certain expertise, you can see that M. Dreyfus is a
man of standing. "Standing" is a word that the French
like to use frequently and in breathy English, their jaws
drooping like a carp's, to signify a mixed bag of achievements: social, athletic, residential, financial and so on.
It appears that M. Dreyfus was a qualifier in several of
these races, not the least of which was political. He had
been elected, six years earlier and again subsequently, to
an important position on the City Council. M. Dreyfus
was one of two Jews in high office in a city known for its
large and prosperous Jewish population since Roman
times, which makes you wonder if history and numbers
have any impact at all. M. Dreyfus was not a marked
man because he was a French Jew, not in the winter of
'39–'40 anyway. He was in danger because he was an
elected Jew who had for years, repeatedly and in the
most public of circumstances, shot his mouth off in crit-
icism of the Nazis, who were rapidly gaining ground and
power. A man of real standing upholds it.

The 3.5-liter Delahaye Type 135M, body by Figoni et
Falaschi, had, André says, impeccable road manners.
André understands these things better than I. She certainly looks like a lady, slim and rich, above reproach in
spite of a rakish hat of striped mattressing fastened to
her roof, and the bulky tank she trails. That tank carried
the Dreyfuses' gas and on top of it I see another mattress.
They were worried about the strafing, naturally. Without
that tank the Dreyfuses wouldn't have gotten far because, souped up as she was, the Type 135M did something in the neighborhood of nine miles to the gallon,
which isn't terrific when there's most of France to cross
between Fontainebleau and Bordeaux and the driving
conditions aren't optimal. Walking was entirely out of
the question because, at the time, Mme. Dreyfus happened to have lobar pneumonia. She wasn't getting pen-
icillin for her pneumonia because its therapeutic effects

had not, at the time, been discovered. As the doctor was quick to point out, it was either go and die or stay and die. Not an impossible choice for a marked man to make. At the time, the Dreyfuses, with thousands of others, were trying to get across the Loire before the French blew up all the bridges, which is what everybody said the French would do. M. Dreyfus had been demobilized two weeks before, at the end of April, which was a stroke of luck, really, because Mme. Dreyfus couldn't drive worth a damn sick or well and a month later might have been a little late. M. Dreyfus had been demobilized because he had just had a birthday that made him too old to fight, technically, and in April of 1940 there still wasn't a war you could call a war going on. They were heading for Bordeaux because it was a seaport and because that's where everybody said the government would relocate if France fell. Those who knew, knew France would fall. They were right about France, right about the bridges, and wrong about Bordeaux. In the photograph, André swaggers on the running board, one arm through the open window and twined around the steering wheel and the other pointing to a pigeon that has made itself comfortable on the long and narrow bonnet of the Delahaye. Behind André, through a rear window, I can see Mme. Dreyfus's pinched face, her dark and anxious eyes staring, her black hair swept up and back in great wings like the fenders of the car. In the trunk of the car, not an ample one, a small suitcase full of gold coins and kilo-size gold bricks lies in unseen but useful splendor. A few bricks account for the tank they trail and more will account for much more. On that trip the Dreyfuses will leave behind themselves a river of gold, tears, sputum and the unpossessable. It was André's job to haul the suitcase from car to lodging place. André's early fiscal exertions under fire will prove, in later years, to have damaged more than his sciatic nerve. The lodging, like the strafing, was more of a miss than hit affair. But with a half-dead woman on his hands and weather that was not with them, M. Dreyfus had at least to try. They spent six days in a château bought for the occasion when Mme. Dreyfus was running a temperature of 41 degrees Celsius and abandoned when her fever broke. André slept in overpopulated chickencoops, in bank vaults, in a monastery and in many barns. His parents, he says, did not sleep much. The picture was taken, André says, when they had to wait by the side of the road at a major intersection near Orléans for nine hours and watch a German convoy proceeding in a westerly direction. André counted 352 trucks and then he stopped counting.

A postcard, whose pre-printed message I have translated freely:

1. (date and place)
2. _____healthy, _____sick.
3. _____lightly, seriously, ill, injured.
4. _____without news of, _____ dead.
5. _____prisoner, _____killed.
6.
7.
8.
9.
10.
11.
12.
13.

André has several of these "family" cards, unused, which his mother found in a pocket that was part of the lining of a valise she brought to this country. Mme. Dreyfus had a supply of these postcards to fill in and send to her mother and her brother in Paris from Vichy, where they were living. André wrote often to his Oncle Philippe but got very few cards in return and, oddly, kept none. These cards were for over a year the only means of communication allowed between what they called the Free and the Occupied zones of France. They did not, these cards, leave much room for matters of a personal nature. Mail and the telephone functioned well enough to the south, where André's family on his father's side was living. The Dreyfuses, Grand-maman Anne included, had all been together on vacation in Saint-Raphaël the summer André was in Dinard, and they stayed south all that time, snug as bugs, in touch.

Three girls in what I know to be the blue uniform coats of a convent school hold hands and stand in a line so straight that it looks like the photographer may have scuffed a mark for them to stand by with his shoetip in the snow that covers the ground. André says he didn't, or doesn't remember. He took the picture in the school-yard, placing the girls to the right of the steps leading up to a door designated "FilleS" in sausagey letters across it. A year later the girls will have had stars sewn onto their blue coats, stars that I know will be yellow, and the yard may turn out to be an exercise yard in Drancy or Royallieu or Les Milles, but for that moment and for now they are indistinguishable from the other convent girls, two of whom are seen in the background, twirling a jump rope. The girls are André's friends in Vichy: Annick, Laure and Danielle. There did not happen to be another Jewish boy in the class that year and these girls were kind enough to go against their pubescent grain and count André in, possibly because no other child cared or dared to. Vichy, where Pétain entertained, was enjoying a tourist boom in 1941 that had little to do with its celebrated waters. As a result, housing and academic opportunities were strictly limited. The best the kilo-size bricks could do was an apartment of two rooms, too small, not far from the only school that would take André in. Companionship and suitability were not even secondary considerations. Half of a nun stands on the left side of the photograph. Half of her mouth turns up in what has to be a smile, half of her coif floats backward in what seems to be a wind although the girls' coatskirts fall smooth enough and their hair, under regulation hats, does not blow. André took the Brownie to school one day in January so he could get a shot of Annick, Laure and Danielle before he left Vichy, which was a thing the Dreyfuses were on the very brink of doing for many months and which they did not actually do for many more. One face, Annick's, frowns in annoyance, with the shutterbugger, perhaps. André says he did not mean for the nun to be in the picture, she just skimmed into his field, although of all the Sisters she was the best to him once he learned to chant the *pater noster* and such-like. In Vichy a lot of prayers were chanted at the most irregular hours. Vichy was the best place to be to apply for, verify, have stamped and countersigned, arrange the transfer to and maybe expedite the arrival of the twenty or so different little pieces of paper which, when fitted together in the proper fashion, might get you some-where. Vichy was the best place to be judged clean and worthy, organically speaking, ideologically speaking, monetaristically, by authentic representatives of coun-tries that might or might not open a door or two, depend-ing on all those papers in their order, depending on some other things. Some of the papers were plain ones like Jewish Census registration cards or the seven kinds of ration cards you needed, and some papers were more difficult like affidavits and entry visas, transit visas, exit visas, danger visas, residence and refugee certificates. Included of course was the standard Gallic glut of birth, marriage, travel, military, medical and vehicular certi-fication. You practically couldn't piss without a special permit in France, where papers often counted for more than the men who carried them. André says his father shuffled and fluttered bits of paper from morning to night and to morning again for the year they lived in Vichy. The trouble was, André says, that some papers expired faster than you could fit others together.

Tante Suzanne, Tante Agathe, Mme. Dreyfus and
Grand-maman Anne occupy the chairs pushed up close
to the tiny iron table that must have been used for breakfast on the balcony. The four women wear print dresses
that could be silk, no sweaters, so it can't be too early in
the season. Behind them, pressed against the railing of
the balcony, are Oncle Felix and Oncle Georges in dark
and natty blazers with a small army of buttons parading
down and over their visible paunches. Behind the railing
is thin air. André says the apartment was six flights up,
which was about as high as you could go in Marseilles
in those days. André and his four Dreyfus cousins are
wedged between the grown-ups in a compositional jum-
ble. I don't think artistic effect was what M. Dreyfus,
taking the picture, had in mind, although there is a nice
if predictable touch in the geranium that intrudes on the
right side of the photograph. Everyone smiles for the
camera, a bit deliberately, too charmingly. André says
his father took the picture just after he had a loud and
prolonged quarrel with his brothers, the women weep-
ing, the children sent downstairs to wait it out. M. Dreyfus wanted his family to leave France with him and he
had come to Marseilles for a weekend in April to persuade
them. Oncle Felix and Oncle Georges would have none
of it. They were in no mood to play emigration games,
not with their properties and their factories and other
similar valuables which, *c'est vrai,* had been Ary-
anized but would one day soon be recoverable. Mean-
while they had, as M. Dreyfus did, small heavy suitcases
with which they could buy time and whatever. What they
didn't have was a mark on their heads. Neither Oncle
Felix nor Oncle Georges had ever been elected to anything more noticeable than the board of directors of the
Jewish hospital in Strasbourg. They had no reason to run
and, as often happens, they tended to ignore the antic
behavior of a younger brother. As often happens, they
should have listened. Grand-maman Anne wanted to
stay because, finally, there were more of her children

staying than going. One child, in the photograph, sits on top of the iron table, her legs hanging down. She can't be more than six. She has socks but no shoes on her feet, typical six, and the springy curls on her head more or less obscure the lower part of Mme. Dreyfus's face. More than less, everyone in this picture was obscured. Of the eleven people I see on the balcony, I have met, apart from André and his mother, only Tante Agathe, who played the piano and sang so amusingly that the German officers at Drancy kept her handy in case they got the blues. The rest of them, without Tante Agathe's talents, were sent from Drancy to Auschwitz to obliteration. The photograph is overexposed, whited out like its subjects. A filter might have done the trick. M. Dreyfus was not used to the Mediterranean light that bleaches hair and bones and leaves the eyes smarting.

On the second day out the weather blew up fast, mashing the May-fat clouds into a mean gray pancake. The boat pitched and yawed and it was all they could do, André says, to keep his mother on her feet long enough for him to run and fetch his father's camera and for M. Dreyfus to find a fellow passenger to snap the three of them around the ring-shaped life preserver. M. Dreyfus figured, rightly, that he wouldn't see much of his wife again until they landed in New York. As the sun was already gone, there are no shadows, no dark spots in the photograph. Everything seems to be of equal value, undifferentiated. The three figures form a triangle of which André is the apex, sitting on the taffrail with his feet propped on the round white ring that reads "S.S. *Exeter* . . . New York." Each parent's inmost arm is around André's back, their fingers creeping forward around his waist to grasp him firmly by the sleeveless sweater he wears. André stretches his arms around his parents' shoulders, embracing them in rigid symmetry. The perfect circle inside the perfect triangle may have some cabalistic meaning but I do not know it. What I see, know, is the most frontal determination: no looking back, no looking sideways at each other, not down nor up but ahead, only ahead, eyes fixed on a future not yet in focus, not yet unfolding. M. Dreyfus's face is corrugated now like the bark of the tree he stood beside in André's earlier picture, ridged with remorse, still confident but not utterly. His mother looks sick again, thin and uncomfortable, terrified. André says he had a pretty lousy trip himself because of the way he ate in Lisbon for the two weeks it took his father to lay out the bribes that were necessary to procure their passage on the *Exeter*. André says he hadn't really been hungry during the two years they were on the move but when he got to Lisbon he just couldn't keep his hands off the white bread. He ate white bread with and between meals and at night, alone in the hotel while his parents were out promenading in the soft sweet air of a coastal city that still permitted promenading in the late spring of 1941. They took long walks, André says, because his mother was unable to sleep without dreaming the kind of dreams you couldn't dream and leave. André says he also ate a fair amount of chocolate, although the Portuguese chocolate was nothing to write home about, and a lot of oil-rich sardines. Together and with the weather, these delicacies lumped and thumped in André's stomach, heaving in syncopation with the tossing of the ship. It took three days for André to throw it all up and then some. The *Exeter* hung on the roll worse than she should have because, belowdecks, she had already been cleared out and converted for usage on what would be her next run, as a troop ship. There were two large sleeping areas, male and female. In the bunk next to André's, on the other side from where his father slept, a boy, maybe nineteen, smoked and cried for long hours. The boy was Polish and incommunicado because there were not, at the time, many Poles sailing and no others on that boat. The regular method of transport for Poles, at the time, was by cattle car. André says he didn't see the boy on deck until the morning of the day they made land, May 28, 1941, a fine day.

Part Three

A Positive I.D.

X

Some people have the most irregular beginnings. They had to have parents, and a childhood, but that isn't where they come from. Do you remember how bright-eyed Athena sprang full-grown from Zeus's brow, giving him one terrible headache as she did so? Connie Jane Steinberg's creation was like that, only there didn't seem to be a suffering Zeus around. I met her the day we both arrived as freshmen at Wellesley and I watched her give birth to herself in slightly less than the regulation nine months. On and off, I've been watching her ever since, drawn like a fly to sugar on the rim of a bowl.

I could never understand exactly how Connie performed that radical amputation of her life before her life. She was eighteen from the start. Beautiful. And smart. And it didn't seem to have cost her anything to get that way. I knew for a fact that she was constantly in touch with her family. I knew because we used to do bells at Wellesley. That meant sitting at the switchboard for an hour or so a week and answering the phones for the whole house. It also meant that everyone knew just who got calls and where, if long-distance, they came from. Connie got a weekly call from her mother in Woodmere on Tuesday nights between eight and nine o'clock, which happened to be my bell hour. She may have heard from her parents more often but not on my time. If it was noisy in the corridor we lived on, Connie would sometimes come downstairs to the telephone closet near the switchboard and I would overhear her part of the conversation. What she had to say to her mother amounted to little more than "no" or "next week" or "A-minus" and they did not speak for very long. I couldn't believe how smooth Connie's face was when she came out of the phone closet. When I finished talking to my mother I was always in tears. Either I missed her or I maligned her, especially that first year.

I came to college so loaded with real and imagined baggage that I scarcely got around to unpacking before my four years were up. My room was as messy as my mind, with books, records and doubts piled high in dusty corners. Connie's room, next to mine on the second floor of Tower Hall, had in it the one bed, one desk, one chair, one lamp and one bureau that the college provided and not much else. Connie hadn't brought anything from home but a trunkful of clothes and the body that fit them. Even that body wasn't to be found in her room very often. Right from the start, Connie was on the make. She must have seen at once that you can't just generate yourself from scratch. You have to find accessible bits from desirable models and then, the trickiest part, you have to synthesize. So Connie spent most of her waking time out of her room: eyes open, ears open, her mind the *tabula rasa* that educators and philosophers drool over.

The raw material, you understand, was all there. Connie had the seamless good looks and great figure that could go in any direction she chose. It's true that her natural coloring limited her somewhat. She would never resemble those long-legged blondes who stalked our cor-

ridors like so many white whooping cranes in a bog. But
Nordic apart, Connie was adaptable. Her true supple-
ness, the one I found so astonishing, so audacious, was
not in her body. Long before conglomeration became a
word we encounter daily in the financial press, Connie
was practicing the kind of takeovers that would have
made Gulf & Western blush for shame. I couldn't wait
from week to week to see what new slouch, which mannerism, what turn of speech or pattern of thought, would
appear, only a touch transformed, in Connie. Connie
used people like lipsticks, blotting them carefully onto
herself before throwing them away. I would have liked
to protest, to tell her that using people uses them up, but
that didn't seem to be the case. The girls whose traits
found their way into Connie's repertoire weren't missing
anything to speak of.

Connie went home for Thanksgiving, she got letters
and phone calls from home, and I knew she had an older
brother nearby, at Tufts, who came to see her once in a
while, but never in all our talk did I get much hard information about her first eighteen years or her family. I
knew her name was Connie Jane Steinberg. Connie, not
Constance: it said so in our Freshman Directory. I didn't
know about her friends at home. I didn't know if she had
ever been to camp or in the hospital or to Europe. I didn't
know if she had ever had braces, piano lessons or sex
before college. I did a lot of heavy guessing and, in spite
of Connie's refusal to divulge what I considered real and
necessary background material, there was plenty to talk
about. Our primary topics were the other girls on our
corridor, Harvard men, a chosen few of our better-look-
ing male professors, and our courses. I should say these
were Connie's topics. I listened. Big talkers like Connie
eat listeners for breakfast, but since there were very few
people I ever listened to besides Connie I didn't feel particularly chewable.

Like Connie, I stayed up late, smoked Parliaments and
played a rotten hand of bridge. If you didn't play bridge

on practically a tournament level you didn't have many social options in those dormitories. Playing bridge and knitting argyle socks took up a serious portion of time in the years I went to college. Inexplicably, we were allowed to knit during classes. Anyone who can take copious notes and knit argyles all at once, and often in the dark, can do anything she puts her mind to. We Wellesley girls were known for our indubitable and overriding efficiency. There were three full-time bridge games on our floor, with players dropping in and out according to their academic schedules and their sanitary needs. On weekends, when the dormitory population was decimated because girls were out delivering argyles to men who were kindly wearing them, the second-string players got a chance. But during the week they never asked us. As Connie was a talker and I was available, more neighborly than not, she made a habit of coming into my room for a couple of hours late every night. And I figured there was another reason she came to talk to me. There was nothing of mine she could possibly want for herself, nothing, so she could try out on me the bits she was appropriating from the other girls. I was never anything to Connie but a moon she shined on, a better mirror than that streaky glass stuck like a postage stamp to the wall above the bureau in her room. If some new gesture or expression worked on me, it was sure to work even more successfully outside my room. Connie was counting in a big way on the proposition that nobody ever seems to recognize themselves in other people.

Well, nobody did, or at least not to complain about. By the time there was deep snow on the ground I could see some shape to Connie's borrowings. Connie was approximating a kind of internationalism that must have been a long way from home for her. There were a large number of foreign girls at Wellesley then, many of them on a French corridor in the attic of Tower Hall, so Connie's source was close at hand. Connie began some vigorous reading in post-War French literature, in French of course. She bought a black cape and wore it over a black skirt when the rest of us were trotting around in Bermuda shorts, our knees red and crusty with the cold. She hung a map of Paris in her room and Simone de Beauvoir was a name she dropped no less than twice a day and not always in conjunction with Sartre either. Connie befriended an Italian girl who was perishing quietly on the floor below us and with whom she went home to Milan over the Christmas vacation. The Italian girl never came back but Connie did and with her came an odd inflection that had modulated her voice to the point where you couldn't be sure that she hadn't learned her English as a French student doing a term at Oxford. Fantastic! By the time the snow had melted Connie had taken, along with the required English 100 and posture classes, one giant step toward the synthesis she was effecting. Connie was engaged to a B. School man. The man's name was Jim Davis and he looked plain but not unattractive; he had glasses and a future, that was clear enough. Jim was due to graduate in June and he had a job waiting for him in his father's Wall Street firm. Jim was considered one of the prize catches of our freshman year, a year in which there were more catches than misses. Connie had met Jim at a Tower Hall mixer in February. I wasn't there that night but I heard that Connie appeared in purple from eyes to feet. By the next afternoon the local drugstore had sold out its small stock of mauve eyeshadow and Jim had called six times. It went quickly from then on and by August they were married. None of us were invited to the wedding.

Connie transferred to Barnard and occasionally I'd call her when I came home to New York on vacations. I went to visit her a couple of times in the large apartment on East 77th Street that she and Jim had furnished, were furnishing, would forever furnish in a constant and restless turnover of the latest thing. I never saw anything move around so fast as the armchairs in that apartment.

Their spare rooms were warehouses of lapsed taste and interests, waiting to become nurseries. One of them did just that after Connie's junior year at Barnard. I saw her early in that summer when I was home. Connie was excessively pregnant. Her big belly swanked through the air like a hot and obstinate breeze. Connie didn't plan to finish college after the baby was born and I could see why, although I thought she was being as rash as the rubella epidemic that she had avoided so carefully six months before. The role Connie had been working on so diligently had moved well beyond any academic instruction. Forgetting the furniture in perpetual motion, Connie's confidence and authority blazed brighter than the silver tray on which she served me tea. She was articulate, urbane, as beautifully dressed as was possible in her amazing condition, and she was less aggressively Continental than she had been. It was definitely a class act. I listened and what I learned from the miscellany of her conversation was that Connie had an impatient and obstreperous interest in power: in getting it and using it and keeping it. They didn't give degrees in power studies at Barnard, not then or yet.

Money, as they say, talks. On its own it isn't that loquacious, it's just pale-green paper folding in on itself, mumbling in a vault. It takes someone like Connie to make money sing. I may have been one of your college all-stars majoring in Indecision with Honors in Confusion but I happened to know plenty about money and power. I come from a long and well-heeled line of powerful men and women about whom the least said is probably best. While power was nothing I had thought about for myself, I had been trained like a hound to smell it anytime and on anybody. I'm not talking about the garden-variety power that has to do with hiring and firing, or about gifts like great strength or wit or artistry. Available power, as I had always known it, consists of paired elements: someone who imposes his will on someone else who concedes to it. No concession, no power. It's a very simple arrangement, one that locks the forcer and the forced into a sinewy constellation of event and assent. That's not necessarily as athletic as it sounds, although wrestling is a part of it, and it isn't just one on one. A powerful person generally has large clumps of followers at his feet, and there can be some fine forces along with the merely imperative ones.

Connie had her baby and I didn't see her again until well after she had had another one and I had produced three of my own. By that time I had spent part of the year after graduation in London, technically and for parental purposes enrolled at the London School of Economics. I had lived in London with an actor I had known in Cambridge, Mass., when we both had ostentatious ideas about careers on the stage, possibly joint careers, that is. My actor took off when the weather and I turned nasty but I stayed on a bit because of that little technicality at the LSE and because I liked it. I managed without too much trouble to postpone writing a thesis, indefinitely. After several months I went home to New York, got a job, met one man and then soon met another who moved me in every sense of the word. Six weeks later I was married and living in Boston for the duration of the two different residencies my husband was to do at Mass. General. By the time I got back to New York on a permanent basis I had three young children and enough of New England forever. I also had a good part-time job waiting for me anytime, my hours, in the New York office of a foundation whose benefactor, a Bostonian, felt much as I did about that astringent city. Or so he confided to me one night at a dinner party in Brookline, when we became soul mates over the consommé.

My husband and I found an apartment, opened his office, and got our oldest child into one of the less predatory private schools. Our reentry into New York life was considerably easier but more time-consuming than we had anticipated it might be. Almost half a year passed before

I got around to reporting for work and, subsequently, to calling Connie, which is a thing I did because I am a congenitally curious person. When we met the following week for lunch I could see that Connie had swooped ahead in my absence. Never mind that old argument about style and substance. Connie's version of the real thing was so acute in detail and finish that it left me gasping, unfortunately with some mussels in my mouth. I choked for a while, using the interlude to count the rings on Connie's fingers. Little rings on long fingers, to be sure, but eight? I had obviously been in Boston too long. Connie had found, after the cape and the purple and the maternity clothes and whatever else hung at the back of her closet, a look which I never saw on anyone else at the time. Connie was swaddled in complex layers of fabric and she rose from her clothes like a fountain. I know it doesn't sound like much but it suited Connie to perfection. She radiated a plashy sexuality that was as eloquent as it was unusual then. But it wasn't just the rings and the clothes that threw me and my mussels into disarray that day, there were other things. One of them was the cast of characters that traipsed through Connie's discourse. Even though I never heard a last name so I'm not entirely sure I knew who everyone was, her message didn't need any decoding. Some people I didn't hear about were Jim and her girls. With the coffee came my understanding of why Connie had bothered to lunch with me at all. It was that job of mine. I wasn't seeing Connie for old times' sake or any other sake you could think of but because Connie had a purpose in mind for me. One of the foundation's special interests was arts funding and of course Connie knew it. It wasn't precisely the first time someone took me to lunch to ask for money but it was the first time I hated it.

Connie had, in the years since I'd seen her, zeroed in on the New York Philharmonic, a worthy if somewhat overstrung orchestra. I had not known Connie to be fond of classical music so I assumed that she had chosen the

Philharmonic because Jim's father was a liberal donor to it. That happy fact opened several doors faster than just knocking on them would. It may have been, too, the various Rockefellers lurking on the premises at Lincoln Center. Where Rockefellers lurk people like Connie will track them, backed up by whole committeeroomfuls of well-bred volunteers whose goals are as brittle and glossy as their nails. Doing good, raising money and your social position at the same time, is one of the easier games in town for anyone with a flair for putting a dollar value on personal relationships. I had never done any volunteer work myself, but my job, just three months of it, had brought me into close and often uncomfortable contact with that ultramondaine flock of females who work so hard for so little, all honking the nonprofit anthem as loudly as geese in an October sky.

Connie informed me that her immediate competition at the Philharmonic was more limp than stiff, and I could tell that she was at a strategic point on a curve that was spiraling upward. Connie was ready to make a quantum leap and what she needed was a boost in the form of equal footing: a trusteeship. Remember Athena? Only this time it looked like I was the bespoke Zeus. What Connie wanted from me was one hundred thousand dollars for a project of hers that, if she handled it right, could be of more than marginal utility. She didn't want to ask Jim's father for that kind of money, she said, and while she didn't mind hustling for it at certain small and select dinners, my arrival in New York with a foundation in what looked like my very own pocket would save her the trouble. I was suddenly stupid. I denied having any substantive say in the matter. I elaborated on the chronic vagaries of the man in Boston. I did everything I could short of walking out of the restaurant to make Connie understand that things, for me, didn't work that way. It took a few months and the figure was slightly reduced but Connie proved me wrong. What Connie wanted Connie got and, to simplify, it really is a worthy orchestra and it really is hard to resist playing God when that rare opportunity presents itself.

It helped. Two years later Connie became a trustee of the Philharmonic. She was young (as those people go), Jewish and a woman, so her nomination was quite a feat in New York, where the cultural establishment likes to ignore that those three traits, in mutable combinations, are what make up the largest number of their paying customers. Connie didn't discard me as she did many of the people she had used. I didn't exactly hold all of the purse strings but I sure held some of them. Connie seemed to need me once more as a mirror for her manners, for her newest self that was much greater than the sum of so many parts. When Connie needed you she couldn't have been more endearing.

And so I became a Connie watcher, again. Like many people, what I felt about Connie was a ripe mixture of outrage and envy. Connie compelled attention like a field full of flowering weeds, colorful and relentless, altogether remarkable. And in spite of Connie's palpable usage of them, her friends kept coming back for more of the same. Maybe they thought that her success would stick like pollen onto their own lives and maybe it did. Unlike many people, I am more than just seasonally allergic to celebrity, so that aspect of Connie's success didn't succeed too well with me. Perhaps if I had understood more about success I could have wanted it more. I mean if a person makes music or Brillo pads or cuts lawns or diamonds or surgical holes in your body, that's product and service for you, identifiable and measurable. That's work that starts and stops and sometimes satisfies: that I can understand and can even admire. But the cooky-pusher's work, my own job for instance, is never done because it's never really done. I filled out some forms and maybe a year later a new dance company gave two performances at the Beacon Theater, for which they had to paper the house. I had no sense of having worked to make those performances. And whose achievement was that, mine or the dancers' or the money-man's grandfather's? Confusion like mine presented a definite occupational hazard, I knew it, and I really should have considered another line of work. Luckily for her, Connie had no such problem defining success for herself. She was so eager to equate celebrity with accomplishment that she never stopped long enough to do the math.

Connie's career went up faster than prefab housing and with some of the same shortcuts. She went to Washington monthly as a member of a national committee on inner-city culture questions. Although she had never graduated, Barnard saw Connie's pecuniary possibilities and made her a trustee. There was scarcely an invitation in New York's febrile benefit life that did not have Connie's name on it. Connie hired a press agent whose job it was to ensure that she made the columns on a frequent enough basis so that it would be worth her while to also hire a clipping service. When the Philharmonic went on its European tours Connie went along as ambassadress and franchised party-giver, at her own expense of course. Connie knew everyone who mattered, straight or gay, performer or patron, in the entire musical world not excluding Russia. In her diverse capacities at the Philharmonic Connie made deals, moved people, commanded a choice army of *shmucks,* picked brains, took credit, and traded up, always up. In the next couple of years I watched Connie become, if you'll allow me a word, hegemaniacal. She fucked power the way other people sometimes fuck each other, for keeps. I mean that both literally and figuratively. By now it was no secret except perhaps to Jim and his father that Connie was systematically and I hoped with some pleasure screwing her way to what she took for the top. You might think that in our pill-assisted and pansexual landscape nobody could really believe that fucking is a road that leads anywhere but to another road. Wrong. For Connie it was still the ultimate sweetheart deal. Unnecessary, maybe, but oh how ultimate.

There was something I spotted in Connie at about this

time that impelled me to see her in another light. It's a thing you don't often come across these days unless you read a lot of Euripides, not really my favorite author, and it may account for my equivocal and continuing interest in Connie. Not justify, just account. Connie had a flaw, an old-fashioned flaw, the flaw of *hubris*. I hadn't seen it at Wellesley and I hadn't seen it in her pushme-pullyou rush to the head of another class. I had been a little slow on the uptake but I saw it now and it unraveled for me that historyless past of hers. Having no past, or being able to cancel out the past you have, implies that the future is also without limits. That's what *hubris* is all about, illimitability. We don't, in our homogenized world, have much room for *hubris* any more. Most of us are punched in and out, engineered and labeled and, shortly, disposable. No one likes it very well but that's where our technology took us, thanks a lot. We rock up and down and out according to the way our blood runs and the tabulated tides of circumstance. When someone like Connie, self-programmed, appears it's bound to make waves of one sort or another. And if that person has a flaw as classic as Irene Papas's profile, those may not be gentle ripples.

Jim gave a party for Connie's thirty-fifth birthday, at what he euphemistically called "21-plus," that was a major blast. That's what the press said and that's what I say, although our takes may have been different. As you enter "21" there's a small paneled and sporting-printed hall that serves as a waiting room for rejects. That evening there were no rejects. One hundred people paraded up the narrow stairs as through Titus's Arch to a room on the third floor that was, by the time we got there, filled with smoke, music, the smell of food and sweet contingencies. Everyone seemed iridescent that night, basking in a Milky Way of their own manufacture, lapping at the Grade A cream of arrival. Even the small talk was *arriviste,* it being February and everyone on their way to or from somewhere else. But it was Connie we were celebrating and she had choreographed the evening in such a way that only an idiot could mistake it. From canapés to conversation, the arrangements had been made beforehand. For example, at our table of ten there were four of us who worked in the floating world of foundations. I saw musicians at another table and photogenic committeewomen with their brisk spouses at another and so on. Ten tables made ten facets of a gem that, in the dim light of "21," sparkled as if it were a real one. Connie moved from table to table, polishing her possibilities like the best of English butlers. She was, as always, brilliantly dressed. Not brightly, of course, but cleverly. White, plain white wool to the floor with a thick rope of pearls at her waist that hung, looped, in the general area of her pubic mound. She looked positively vestal, which is just the right look for a birthday girl celebrating such a nice round number. It was a terrific evening, in spite of the compartmentalization of the guests and Connie's inhospitable reluctance to introduce members of different categories to each other. Even my husband, who tends to break out in hives when I so much as mention Connie to him, had to admit it was a good party.

We've all seen spaceship launchings on television. As the rockets ignite and the vehicle lifts off the pad, part of the gantry bursts into strings of fire, consumed by what it supported. That's just about what happened, soon after that party, to Connie and Jim. Jim may have shuddered and groaned for a while but when Connie's payload was really up there and she didn't need him, their marriage collapsed as publically as any gantry does. Fifteen years, two children, six fat scrapbooks of assorted clippings and a prominent place in some people's universe was what that marriage amounted to for Connie. Connie must have thought it was time for her to move on to something grander, something nobler, something along the lines, say, of an Italian *principe*. I don't think Connie knew it but she was way off course. That old devil *hubris* had

been jamming her signals for a long time and where
there should have been beams there were blind spots.
There's no other explanation for why she made the mis-
takes she was much too smart to make. Understand that
nothing cataclysmic occurred. War and nature apart,
nothing cataclysmic ever does. There's just a shift, a rift,
and it's over.

When Jim had finished picking up the charred lumps
of pride that were left to him, he turned around and got
stunningly assertive. A little *post facto* but I think his
father and the lawyer may have had a say in that. Jim
asked for and got the girls. He didn't have to go to court
for them because as it turned out Connie didn't want
custody of her children, but Jim was preparing for a
court fight to end all court fights. I know because he
called to ask me if I would, if it came to that, testify on
his behalf. I said I wouldn't. I never heard from him
again. In the spirit of overkill, Jim asked the same question of so many people in New York that he could have
staffed a few of the firm's branch offices with everyone
who said no as I had. Outrage and envy notwithstanding,
there was something in Connie you couldn't testify
against. It did not seem safe or reasonable to do so. Connie managed to get the apartment and a sum of money,
in lieu of alimony, that was rather less than she'd intended but enough to keep her from being distressed for
a number of years. She was required, in exchange for
this sum, to stop using Jim's name. It couldn't have been
easy for Connie to be shoved so dramatically back into a
Steinbergian dusk but she was fresh out of choices.
Begin countdown. Miscalculation number one: the back-
fire effect.

With some of the money, Connie rented a small and
tidily restored farmhouse outside of Florence, in Harold
Actonsville, that matched the small and elegant man
with her in the photographs she sent me many months
later. One picture, taken in a narrow-looking garden in

front of the house, shows Connie and her dapper fellow sitting at a table. Behind them stand two footmen wearing the striped jackets that footmen wear in Tuscany when they aren't wearing livery. Below the table lies a large and spotted dog. It was the kind of photograph that oozes well-being through every grainy pore. The letter that accompanied the photos said, redundantly, that she was fine and would be back in New York after the summer. Connie wrote that the house was called "Villa Favorita" but she did not identify the man who appeared to go with the house.

As I happened to go to the hairdresser one day in September and happened to pick up a copy of *Women's Wear* that had been left on a chair, I learned that Connie was back in town. She had been photographed at the opening night of the opera. On her arm was that same man, named now for me in the caption as Dieter von und zu Hohenfels. Von und zu: a double-barreled species of aristocrat whose natural habitat is Germany and whose normal feeding habits do not include divorced Jewesses. I would have found out anyway because a month later my husband and I were invited to a cocktail Connie gave in honor of Dieter von und zu. There was a tiny coat of arms embossed at the top of the invitation card. Connie's name in flowing script ran right below it. She was anticipating.

My husband would not go to the party but I did, only to discover that Dieter was not what I had expected him to be. In the few minutes I had alone with him I could see immediately that Dieter wasn't one of those heel-clicking, hand-kissing automatons whose bright blue eyes drill holes through the people they consent to look at. Okay, okay, so Germans make me nervous: it's in my genes. Dieter was almost twenty years older than Connie and me and he looked it, especially in and around his exophthalmic eyes. He had, as Connie told me later, a deep and beneficent involvement with Wagner's music as it is performed at Bayreuth, which is where she met him. Dieter was, surprise, a mystic. A vegetarian, non-sectarian, hyperventilating bachelor mystic. Nowadays, mystics are as common as cockroaches: everybody has a few in their lives. Chanting mantras and biofeedbacking, the troops mass for a psycho-Babelized assault on the banality of their private and merely physical selves. A little introspection goes a long way these days. But several years ago when all of this was taking place a man who was both numinous and communicative was, in the Western world, hard to come by. And a spiritualist with a coat of arms, a large fortune (the German nobility are rarely impoverished, Connie was no fool), and a damp but livable *Schloss* on the Rhine was another prize catch for Connie. She would have to take a bit of transcendentalism along with the title, but that surely wouldn't disturb her.

Connie spent most of that winter in New York with and without Dieter at her side. I think he was in Germany some of the time clipping coupons, or deep-breathing with his guru and his tailor in London, or doing whatever it was that a man like Dieter did from day to day to fill up a life. I saw Connie for lunch one day after the party. Connie told me that Jim had sent the girls away to Rosemary Hall, not at all against their wishes, and that he was living with a girl who couldn't be too long out of boarding school herself, or out of Katharine Gibbs anyway. The young lady was Junior League and mainly junior, a fact that stung Connie like a nettle. I had never seen her so ruffled, so sulky. In one long expository sentence Connie told me that she was going to marry Dieter and that he was, annoyingly, a part-time homosexual. She also told me, in what was for her a rare confessional vein, that the Philharmonic could go shove it up their asses if they thought she'd resign from the Board just because they'd asked her to. It seemed that Jim's battle plan during their divorce proceedings had been even more extensive than I realized at the time. Connie was devalued in a variety of ways. Cash-and-carry is the pol-

icy on most nonprofit boards and Connie's cash was nowhere near enough to carry her, especially when Jim's
father withheld his generous donation for reasons which
he did not withhold. Connie, in her powerful thrust to the
top, hadn't covered her trail as a good girl should. There
were too many people who knew too much. In spite of
what looked like Connie's kinky but substantial expectations, they didn't want any part of her on a regular basis.
Miscalculation number two: nobody loves you for your
overefficient self.

A postcard came from Connie and Dieter, who were in
Bayreuth in August. As they spent all of the next winter
in Europe, I didn't see Connie again until the following
November. They stopped in New York for a few days on
their way to Arizona. Dieter had a new holy man who
was living in the desert and allowing a few disciples to
live with him for a not-just-nominal fee. They weren't
married yet and when I asked Connie why, she gave me
an imprecise discourse on contemporary sexual mores.
What she said sounded like garbage to me. I knew Connie and I knew what she wanted and it wasn't free and it
wasn't love. What I couldn't figure out was why Connie
hadn't left Dieter and found herself a likelier berth. Connie's position in New York had eroded, partially by attri-
tion, but her money couldn't have run out yet. As our
conversation progressed I understood some part of Connie's uncharacteristic passivity. That wasn't just
Dieter's holy man in the sand. Chameleonic as ever, Connie had really outdone herself this time. She told me that
she spent her days in deepest meditation. She fasted, had
visions, heard voices, spoke in tongues: the parapsycho-
logical works. Connie wasn't up to bending spoons by
thinking them bent but she was, she insisted, totally in
touch with her essence, her life force. More garbage.
Connie had no essence. There was no single, central person who lived and moved in the muddle of all those ap-
propriations. Like the Collyer brothers and their mess,

Connie's accumulation filled many rooms but it was worthless, all worthless. And the strongest force in Connie's life was the forcible way she acted on other people. That's the very opposite of a life force. If Connie hadn't been so bamboozled by her *hubris*, she wouldn't have made miscalculation number three. She would have learned, as the rest of us have, that using people uses you up. Another thing that dawned on me, finally, was that Connie and Dieter were habituated to hallucinogenic drugs. Things fell into place and a little out of my reach.

I got a call for help from Connie, who was in New York Hospital three months later. I thought at first it might be a drug-related illness but it wasn't. Connie had checked herself in for a two-week surgical orgy. There was hardly an inch of her skin that hadn't been rearranged. She had been pinched, kneaded, poked and prodded, lifted and flapped and tucked like play-dough in an anxious toddler's hands. Connie told me that she had wanted to get it all over at once and that, something being on a cusp somewhere, the time was right. I thought it was a little early myself, neither of us being that near forty yet. There are some pretty hungry doctors around but Connie's cosmetic surgeon must have been on a starvation diet when he agreed to perform so many operations on one body in so short a time and for such an insufficiency of reasons. Connie showed me her breasts, thighs, ass and eyes and said they were puffy but promising. To me it all looked like macaroni and not more manageable. Seeing Connie, I understood that what was plastic about this kind of surgery was the patient. Non-biodegradable, Connie wouldn't let a little thing like life wear her down. She must have thought she was on her way back to square one: a funny preparation for what should have been an endgame. Connie said she needed me to do some shopping for her. She planned to go straight from the hospital to the Caribbean for a tan to cover the scars with and none of her bikinis would fit because of the redistri-

bution of her masses. Dieter was in London and had said
he would meet her in Jamaica. He didn't know about the
operations and Connie did not intend to point out the new
features on her revised map. In fact, she said, she hadn't
called anyone but me and she expected me to keep my
trap shut about all of this. I did. I ran Connie's errand
and I kept Connie's secret, until now, not because I felt
sorry for her but because I felt obliged, a feeling which
strikes me from time to time and often when I least expect it. I felt I had to see Connie through the crash and
clatter of the storm that was gathering above her lifted
face. Since duty is invariably a one-way street, Connie
didn't feel at all obliged about keeping in touch with me
and I didn't see her again for two years.

Connie went nova, for me, one night in Phoenix with
the terminal flare that I know predicates a collapsing
star. I was visiting my parents, who were in Arizona for
the winter, and I saw Connie in a restaurant. She was
with a group of what could only be called young people
at a big round table. They were dazzling, all be-jeaned
and be-Navaho-jeweled, booted and fringed and frosted
with the blondest hair, their eyes glazed by the sun and
probably something else. I think Connie saw me but she
did not get up until I started to make my way toward the
big table. As I approached, she skittered into the ladies'
room. On the door was a decal of a saguaro cactus wearing a skirt and a hat with blue daisies on it. I followed
Connie into that malodorous place and we sat together
for less than ten minutes on a ledge that ran across a
wall of mirrors. Above us, pink fluorescent tubes sparked
and quivered, fusing Connie and me in the flattest,
harshest light I ever saw. Connie, post-op, looked among
other things like a candidate for a substantial rebate
from the surgeon who had performed such short-term
magic on her. Connie told me that Jim was married to
his junior miss, which was no news to me, as I read the
papers daily. She didn't tell me another thing that I also

knew. Dieter was back in Germany living with a boy whose operatic aspirations were being tuned to the jingle-jangle of the coins in Dieter's pockets. Connie's mouth leaked syllables about one of the people at her table, a painter whose future she was financing in return for a share in it. Connie's words were so out of sync with what I saw in her pink-lit face that I had trouble hearing her. I got the idea all right but I didn't get much beyond that.

I sat on that ledge and listened to Connie for the last time. She was crazed and cracked like some ancient Indian pottery I had seen in the museum that morning. The particular piece I was thinking of had been broken so many times that the label on the glass case it was in read "Vessel: of indeterminate use." I haven't seen Connie again. I have just one thing to say about trying, as Connie did, to simulate being young. Don't bother. It doesn't work. There's nothing prime about starting up. It's the homestretch that counts in any scheme, grand or simpler, and home is only a hole in your head that houses something Connie never kept. That was her first and final miscalculation: she had no fallback position. Connie: princeless and powerless, her girls now women who wouldn't see her, the Philharmonic and "Villa Favorita" light-years away, hollowed out, absurd, hanging on

XI

My sister married a man who painted budget portraits from time to time. As a sideline, he taught. A very occasionally employed artist with extravagant personal habits, that's Benjamin Arthur in a nutshell, which is where I always maintained he belonged.

Benjamin Arthur: I keep waiting for the third part of that name to come out but it never does. Along with a mysterious no-name, Ben's ancestors had passed down to him a misleadingly Irish aspect, although in his speech, his politics and in fact he was as Jewish as they come. Of medium height, black-haired and green-eyed, wonderfully pale, Ben looked as if he might very well know how to handle a shillelagh, which is a thing I can't even spell right the first time. My sister fell immediately, she said, for the fog that Ben made around himself. I don't know whether she thought her warmth would burn off Ben's mist or if she found it something cool for her to hide in, a relief from the sallow, Semitic hyperbole that blows its hot and ambitious breath in our direction.

147

Ben's handiwork dots our family landscape. During the years they were married, the rest of us were encouraged to find ourselves in dynastic moods. Portraits of children, parents, grandparents variously grouped and ranked all bear witness to Ben's way with a palette knife. It's Ben's professional signature, that spiny crust of color that separates figure from ground, feature from face. In his student days he was much admired for it. Ben's paintings are more dark than light and when you saw them massed on the walls in one room, as in my sister's house, it was like being in a grotto: hushed and muggy, dim, implicit.

Ben and my sister lived in an apartment on Riverside Drive near Columbia, which my sister attends systemically. My sister takes courses the way other people take medicine and for the same reason: to feel better. Certain subjects she requires for her head, certain others for her heart, and so on down. Sometimes she studies as a matriculant, other times not. If she lived in Europe where these things count, and if she carried the calling cards which count even more, her little square of pasteboard would be covered over with alphabetical insignia of achievement. Philosophy, Anthropology, Urban Planning, Comparative Literature: you name it and my sister's done at least some of it. My sister has the smarts and can usually rack up a degree in less than the two or three years it takes everyone else. She has been known (but not by any Registrar's Office) to work on two degrees at once. She went straight from college into her graduate regalements. Summers she regularly spent in schools. My sister is as attractive as she is academically immoderate, which is to say very. Her name is Monique. She is a younger sister and of course I used to call her Monkey.

Monique is an identical twin. Her other half, my second sister, lives in Main Line lotus-land to the tinkling accompaniment of the Paoli Local. Her name is Martine and that is what I always called her. Years ago I thought of Monique and Martine as a double-scoop cone that I, older, could lick or not as I chose. I mostly chose to do so, if for no other reason than to exercise personally those divine attributes of the Jewish almighty, wrath and vengeance. They were my people, I was their God, they had none other. It was terrific while it lasted. Monique and Martine look alike, both slim, both shiny, but they do not live or think alike because Martine is older than Monique by fifteen important minutes. Martine is rich in her marriage, rich in children, rich in her professional life as Philadelphia's up-and-coming lady trial lawyer, rich in friends. She does not need or use the income from her trust fund. She does not need or use Monique. That's the kind of an edge that fifteen minutes can give you.

Monique met Ben during the riots at Columbia in the spring of 1968. Ben was teaching part-time at the School of Fine Arts on 110th Street. They found each other, trapped together, in one of the passages that tunnel below the broad and rather grassless plain around which the older buildings of the University are situated. Low Library, Hamilton and Fayerweather were occupied and the ways to Jay and Butler impassable. After several overlong hours a Puerto Rican youth who was definitely not college material came down to evacuate the tunnels. By then Ben and Monique were what can be called an item; she befogged and he kindled by prospects he could only guess at. Monique was twenty-seven and Ben forty, each of them spouse- and childless, both in wholesale sympathy with the revolution that was taking place above their heads. They married perhaps more quickly than was altogether necessary.

When you come from a large and elaborately reticulated family like ours, there's nothing like the thought of an orphan to cheer you up. Ben was an only child with dead parents and one cousin living in Milwaukee and another one in Denver. Period. You couldn't ask for anything less. Neither cousin appeared at the wedding, which took place in early June right after Monique handed in a term paper to what was left of her current department. Ben's guest list, not long, read like a Who's Has-Been in American painting. For reasons that may or may not have to do with talent and timing, Ben and his friends had all fizzled in the wet of unkeepable promise. That bunch was so bitter they made Concord grapes taste like halvah. I know. I listened to them. They all made a beeline for me because along with being Monique's sister, I worked for a foundation whose generosity to artists is rather well-known.

My father is a big provider. When Ben asked for six thousand dollars in cash so that he could spend the summer in France with Monique in the style to which he was about to accustom her, my father was only momentarily appalled. Gifts to daughters can be the shrewdest investments if you live long enough to collect on them. Monique did not, she told me later, know about this transaction until she was in Paris. My father, not wanting to make waves that might swamp the bridal boat, hadn't told my mother or Monique a thing. Monique is not the most practical person. Naturally, they spent all of the money, which is not such a difficult thing to do. Ben's idea of adequate nourishment in France ran to at least six Michelin stars a day, counting lunch and dinner of course. Nothing foggy about that.

Back in New York by Labor Day, Monique and Ben soon found and moved into the place on Riverside Drive. They kept Ben's infrequently used studio room on Christopher Street in the Village. Monique enrolled for yet another year at Columbia, barely taking time to move her mountain of books and her two canaries from my parents' apartment, where she had been living up to her wedding day. My parents were not sorry to see any of the above leave their home and care. Monique, so deep into Byzantine Civilization that semester that she didn't bother to look beyond Justinian's nose, left the furnishing of the apartment to Ben, who had no portrait commissions to occupy him just then. Although he taught a life class twice a week at the Art Students League and although he dropped into my office on a schedule that was distressingly regular, Ben really had little else to do but putter with his new opportunities. He did quite a job. Never has so much been spent on what looked like so little, and in a rental.

A year later, still commissionless, Ben had finished the apartment. Almost every wall, window and water pipe had been tampered with. Bathrooms had leapt across halls with the ease of gazelles, closets expanded, windows and doorways enlarged majestically, spotlights peeped from half-lidded eyes sunk in the ceilings, and there were walls that curved at and away from you like Dr. Caligari's finest. My husband and I were invited one evening to celebrate the departure, at long last, of various and nefarious subcontractors. Before dinner we stood with our drinks at one of the new windows watching the sun set over the Jersey marshes. As it did so, the lights on the roller coaster at the Palisades Amusement Park and on the bridge came out. It could have been a limpid urban moment but Ben's running commentary dulled it for me. We ate our dinner perched on scratchy cushions strewn across the floor. Ben did not believe in furniture as those of us with occasional low-back pain know it. Floor to ceiling, the straighter walls were hung with paintings, Ben's and friends'. I look at a lot of pictures and the second-rate makes me nervous. Monique, who has the visual equivalent of a tin ear and does not demand anything like retinal satisfaction, seemed happy in the space that Ben had made for her. She did not mind, she said, typing her papers in the kitchen on the small chopping-block table that was, besides the bed, the only piece of furniture designed with the human body in mind. And what's more, she said, she adored eating in bed. Hint, hint: connubial bliss. I got it, kid. Monkey.

At this point my father intervened, which is a thing he does when sufficiently provoked. He set up a meeting between Monique, who cut a class to get there, Ben, and his lawyer. My father does not like talking money to his children, so he uses lawyers as go-betweens. As what most lawyers have to say is generally inaccessible except to other lawyers, only Martine has some clear understanding of our mutual financial arrangements. Monique and I know that there is a trust fund, whose principal we can't touch until we're forty, and that the income from it is enough to keep us from asking further questions. We have, as they say, no need to know. My brother has no trust fund because my brother gets the business. Quite standard, I believe. The purpose of the meeting my father set up, as my mother detailed it for me in a conversation so lengthy that we certainly broke all the local telephonic records, was to make Ben appreciate the fact that the honeymoon was absolutely over. My father developed a sudden paralysis of the hand he used to reach into his pocket with. No more gifts. No more renovation. Forget St. Moritz for Christmas. No more cases of Pétrus, six at a throw. No more fur-lined raincoats size 41 Long to ward off Ben's perpetual chills. All expenses were to be reasonable, accountable, and were to be covered by income, earned or unearned, preferably the former, preferably Ben's. What my parents really wanted was no more joint account, but my father hesitated, again, to rock a boat he had no wish to sink.

About love. It existed, for Monique, I'm sure of it. Love is a private shorthand, the marks some people make in books that they open or close. I can't read Monique's marks and you can't read mine. All we see are side effects, by-products, from which we infer cause. It's rudimentary logic. I saw Monique get taller, which was quite a trick at her age. That's all I saw.

I guess Ben caught my father's drift. Christopher Street was dismantled and Ben moved his easels and turps into what wasn't being used as a dining room anyway. At Monique's urging, he called Columbia and was rehired for his job, which had, as so many did, dissipated in the inky aftermath of student revolt. Using my mother as a mouthpiece, Monique convinced selected aunts, uncles and cousins that a portrait was just what was missing in their lives and decoration schemes. Martine, my brother and I had already spoken for ours, of our several children: safe enough. During the following three years Ben painted up a storm of portraits in which the faces bear a greater-than-family resemblance to one another. The money came in more promptly than is usual and Ben's fees were not discussed, also unusual. Monique kept on with her studies.

After all the portraits were made that would be made, after a summer spent in a borrowed house on Nantucket where the light is good, after the scrutiny suggested by that good light and the fact of having passed her thirtieth year a while back, Monique examined her options and came up with a plan. She would work. Ben was teaching, doing his particular best. The income from the trust rolled in quarterly but not as abundantly as it had when the dollar bought almost a dollar's worth of goods. It was time.

For the first September that she could remember, Monique did not go out and get new notebooks, pens, lined yellow pads and the rest of the equipment that is crisper than any air in autumn. It was, she told me, harder than giving up smoking, which was a small but tender economy that she was affecting. Monique registered at several employment agencies and called up everyone she knew in the academic underworld all over New York and vicinity. Jobs were tighter than the braces we used to wear on our teeth and not much more attractive. Selling at Bloomingdale's was out! Ben said so and we all agreed. In December, a kindly editor at an inferior publishing house told Monique what passed for a truth. Monique was as overqualified as was possible for the kind of job that, never having worked, she could get. It is true, I suppose. All those subjects, that heap of facts and fictions ingested and extruded, had prepared Monique for little more than writing the catalogue for the Columbia

School of General Studies. Which if it is a job was not available. Monique persisted, went on interview after interview. In the place of Beethoven's Late Quartets, Monique was taking three credits in Humiliation and Rejection that semester. By the end of January I told Monique that she could work as a receptionist in my office for a couple of days a week, which we both knew was not one of my brighter ideas. In March, in desperation, she let herself get pregnant.

Having babies, like building new houses, brings out the worst in couples. If the worst is not too bad there's a chance, what with the novelty and all, of carrying it off. Monique did not see that Ben, at forty-four, was the baby in his life. Having so recently been given new toys, Ben had no intention of sharing them. Had Monique seen that, or maybe if she had not been so sapped, so crumpled, by the discovery of her apparent uselessness, she would probably have agreed to the abortion that Ben asked her to have right after she announced to him that she was six weeks gone. I also told her to have an abortion and so did Martine, although our line of reasoning did not quite parallel Ben's. Monique was suddenly mulish, a mood that often garnishes an obstetrical situation. My parents, in ignorance of Ben's request, were delighted with the notion that, now, all their children would have children. They are very ongoing people, my parents.

Ben left for England when Monique was well into her third month and it was clear that an abortion would not take place. He went first-class on the QE II, a nice way to go, assuring Monique that he would certainly be back for the birthday. He also took a nice sum of money with him, although he claimed he had a job waiting at the Slade School in London. The first thing Monique did was to go out and buy herself a chair to sit in. The second thing she did was to call Martine. Madame Expert gave her, gratuitously, a legal definition of desertion. My parents were no longer delighted.

Martine came up to New York the next weekend and

called a sisters' conference. We met in the bar of the
Sherry Netherland Hotel. Martine, ironical always,
picked the spot. It is a locale that has some meaning in
our sorority. The first time we three witches met in that
dim cave was on a November afternoon twelve years
earlier, my wedding day. On our way from the hairdresser to the woman, waiting, who was to dress us at
the Pierre, under whose roof I was wed, we detoured for
a couple of liquid and illicit hours at the Sherry Netherland bar. When we finally arrived where we were supposed to have been all along, my mother was red with
rage, a color that did not happen to go well with her
dress. I'll remember it always. On the day of Martine's
wedding and again on Monique's, we reenacted our my-
thology. It's one of our better rituals. And there we were
again, talking matrimony again, all of us older, possibly
even reversible.

We decided that afternoon that Monique would go
down to Ardmore for the rest of her term. With no experience as a live-alone, and with a pregnancy that was
proceeding more bloodily than beautifully, Monique was
uneasy about staying on Riverside Drive. Martine would
be working through the summer and so would be home.
Monique could, if she wanted to, watch the two small
boys in the pool all day, although there was someone paid
to do precisely that. In the evenings, between briefs, they
would be together. Martine's husband, an architect who
travels constantly, was not consulted. Had Martine
called him, he would not have objected to this plan.
Going back to our parents' house did not really come into
consideration. I was excused because I take my children
to Europe every summer to visit their paternal grandmother, have an apartment with no room to spare, and
am not a twin.

I went for a weekend late in August to spend a few
days with Monique in Ardmore after I got back from Europe. I had seen, a week before in a gallery in Basel, a
small watercolor by Derain in which a woman sits in a

Fauve garden. Wedges of blue, orangey-red and green make trees and sky. A figure, more suggested than depicted, wears a yellow dress that slants across the upper half of her body. Monique in Martine's garden was just so fluorescent. Her face had unfolded, the layers laid back to reveal the radiant bone beneath the skin. Like the prize rose at a flower show, Monique was outsized and overcolored, a bit unreal, insolently first. The staining had ceased to be a problem and Ben, not having answered the letters Monique wrote to him at the Slade, did not appear to exist. My nephews' heads when I kissed them smelled of summer, the end of it, a compound of chlorine, talcum powder, citronella, bubble gum and boredom.

When the children went off to school in September Monique moved back to New York. Martine did not stand in her way. Monique had swallowed, as she told me, more of the land of milk and honey than she could possibly keep down in her condition. And if she never saw bleeding madras patchwork pants again it would not be a deprivation. We are not, any of us, what you might call club-prone. Martine can live well in Ardmore because she leaves her head in Philadelphia every night. My parents were by then back from the Swiss mountaintop on which they have passed every August in living memory (with time out for War and East Hampton). They did not insist, as we had thought they might, that Monique come home to have her baby. They must have felt that it was time for her to be on her own. I suppose that's how they saw, most dreadfully, a life for her. It's odd how quickly Ben vanished from everyone's thinking. It's odd because the way Ben does not believe in furniture is the way we do not believe in divorce, in our family. It's unnecessary, unesthetic, probably unhealthy, certainly unnatural. I could go on.

Monique had her baby in December, on my son's birthday, as it happened. The congruency of it tickled my children. A tiny girl, black-haired and uncommonly fuzzy,

Monique named her Ariadne. Not for Ariadne as assistant maze-mapper, she said, but for Ariadne as abandoned, on Naxos. I guess Monique forgot about those Dionysian revels that followed, on Naxos. We all tried to dissuade Monique from doing a child in with a name like that but she would not listen. Ben had not returned, as more or less promised, and judging from that name, Monique must have been as punctured by his absence as she had been transfixed in his presence.

The New Year came and so did Ben, with a story about having been very ill on holiday in the Veneto, far from a functioning telephone and farther from reason because of a high fever and incompetent medical attention. And anyway, he said, he thought the baby was due at the end of January. Since when did Ben have a problem with counting? Ben hadn't received any of Monique's letters. His job in London had fallen through and he had gone immediately to Naples, where he knew some people. The Slade hadn't forwarded his mail. He said he had called Riverside Drive a few times during the summer but when there was no answer he assumed Monique had closed the place up and gone with my parents, where he knew she was in good hands. Since the summer Ben had been busy in Rome doing lucrative portraits in pencil for a multiplex Roman clan whose most lustrous young ornament he had met on the beach in Ischia in July. He was glad to be back. The baby was exquisite. And what kind of classical shit was a name like that? A little late, Benjy sweetie.

Takers take, givers give, users use losers. There's always a dichotomy in two-step time, a dippy dance to the tune of supply and demand. I'm a giver, like Monique, and yet I've learned that to say no is to survive. I mean you can't just let yourself be played upon any old way whenever. There are moments, even years, when you have to go against your grain and say no. It's difficult but not impossible. Martine, who has that edge, is more taker than taken, always was. The trouble is that Monique sees, saw, herself as she sees Martine, who is identical to her, right? What they share are chromosomes and that's all, but try to tell Monique that. When we talked, she insisted that she knew what she was doing, that she had control, even primacy, in her marriage. Speaking evidentially, I'd award that trophy to Ben.

She let him back into her life. It was that simple. As ineffectual as we had been, Martine and I, in the way of nomenclature, so were we useless in the matter of separation papers. Family principles to the contrary, what Monique needed was a good dose of divorce, like salts, like her courses, to clean her out. Monique would not agree. A real father, she said, is better than another and far better than none. A moot point. And, as I said before, I'm sure she loved him. That yellow fog came in again on Ariadne's little feet and sat, silent.

Monique did everything that modern mothers are supposed by the media to have left behind in a dank world of pre-liberation and inconvenience. She nursed Ariadne until the baby bit deep into her nipple one day, she mashed her own baby food, went to Riverside Park morning and afternoon for as honest air as you can get in New York, sewed Marimekko pinafores and comforters, sang, rocked and giggled with Ariadne to a point that was not totally charming any more. For Monique, Ariadne was a measure of her own significance and Ben was its instrument. It was, she told me, a good time for her. And Ben seemed to be as engrossed with the fact of Ariadne as he had been remote from the probability of her. He sketched Ariadne incessantly. They were wonderful drawings, each line informed, restrained, careful. I think he really loved that baby and I think something else. Ben had feared an infringer and what he found was an enhancer, who just also happened to be a meal ticket without any holes punched yet. I also think that for Ben Monique was no more than a funnel that had to be kept in working order, oiled occasionally, whatever you do to funnels to keep the juices running through them.

In April Ben bought a house in Bridgehampton. He and
Monique had driven out to look for a summer rental and
the agent, no hick, had smelled a sale and was quick to
make it. On Ocean Road, the house was about as swell
as you can get in Bridgehampton: white pillars, winding
driveway, potato field and all. Ben said it suited him and
would be good for Ariadne, and he sent Monique to my
father and the lawyer for permission to break into the
trust somehow. Ben and my father locked horns in a battle that reverberates still in the valleys of my mother's
mouth, mostly because Ben won it.

All summer Monique and Ben lived in the rubble of
another reconstruction. Room by room, the workmen
cannibalized the old house and left in its stead a structure pierced by the great sheets of glass that were its
most striking feature. The pillars stayed, but four copper
beeches with knobby knees and branches that hung to
the ground were cut down. Ben wanted vistas and he got
them. Monique, occupied with Ariadne sitting, crawling,
squeaking and leaking, did not pay much attention to
Ben's edificial excess.

If you have a house, you need a car. If you have a car
to take you to the house, you probably need a pool. If you
have a car to take you to the house so you can swim in
the pool, you undoubtedly need a tennis court. So it goes
and so, over the next few months, it went. And it's not
true that the cheese stands alone, because there are always houseguests.

I did Thanksgiving. I usually do. My children like an
assembled family under our roof, a mustering of unques-
tionable closeness that seems to charge them up for
days. The fact that Ben and my mother were barely
speaking did little to reduce the noise produced by seven
children under the age of twelve in a medium-size dining
room in which two and a half sets of permissive grandparents sat. Ben had painted minute animals in a broad,
leafy border around the hem of Ariadne's white smocked
dress, gilding his lily. Ben told me, during an all-too-
short lull, that he had gotten two jobs in Southampton,

from an elderly couple he and Monique had met at the
end of the summer. In order to activate what he hoped
would be a picturesque chain reaction, he and Monique
planned to spend more time in the country. The house
was really ready now, really.

Ben was right about one thing leading to another and
he soon had commissions more geriatric than he might
have liked but at least he was working. I can just see
those old people passing time and their money out there,
waiting for Ben to fix them in a dark and final likeness.
Ben was still teaching, but only two classes and both in
the middle of the week, so he and Monique were not in
New York more than one night a week. I didn't get to see
Monique very much that winter but we spoke often on
the telephone. Rather: I listened to long accounts of Ariadne's every step and syllable. Monique wasn't just involved in motherhood, she invented it.

If I were more mechanical, the particulars of the rest
might not elude me. Twenty minutes outside of New
York on the Long Island Expressway on a morning in
July a small farm truck delivering strawberries suffered
an unspecified malfunction and rammed into the back of
Monique's car when she slowed down because there was
a sudden knot of cars ahead. Ariadne popped like toast
out of the baby seat and hit her head on the windshield.
It was an old car seat, one I had passed down to Monique,
and the straps were missing. By the time the ambulance
got to Elmhurst General the child was dead of internal
bleeding. Monique was alone with Ariadne when it happened. She thought she was pregnant again, which she
was, and had driven in from the country to see her doctor. Ariadne came along because Ariadne always went
along but Ben, whose classes were over for the season,
had no reason to leave Bridgehampton and two sittings
scheduled. I was in Europe. So were my parents. I can
not imagine how that day went by for Monique and
maybe it didn't. I saw the before and I saw the after. By

late afternoon Ben, Martine and my brother were at the hospital and the rest of us were on our way back. For babies, they make tiny white coffins, like toy boats. You send white flowers and not a lot of people come to the funeral; it isn't done.

A week later Monique went into the hospital for a voluntary abortion. She did not want, she said, to replace Ariadne. A week after that she astonished us all by asking Ben for a divorce, which was something he was unwilling to give her. Monique went to Switzerland with my parents for the remainder of the summer and when she got back in September she went out to buy notebooks.

The lawyers did their jobs and by the following summer the promise of a divorce had been extracted from Ben like the rottenest tooth: for a price, it came out quickly. The price was the house in Bridgehampton, which was cheap enough.

Monique still lives in the apartment on Riverside Drive. She is taking courses, this year, in Classical Archeology. She has Latin and Greek, all the prerequisites. Another thing she has, which helps, is tunnel vision. Monique sees straight ahead. That's how she sees.

XII

I watch birds, regularly. On weekends, on vacation, a pair of binoculars hanging on a leather strap around my neck, I'd walk hours in the hope of adding "a new life" to the list I have been keeping since I married. It was my husband, André, a birder since boyhood, who showed me the ropes. I like the quick and the quiet of it. Spot, focus, identify and it's finished in a minute. It's a neat way to make some sense of the part of the world you live in. We're not too good, either of us, with birdsong. We don't seem to hear well enough the different trills, catches and whistles and we miss a lot of birds that way. I mean we hear them but don't know them, can't say for sure that they are what we think they might be. Misses, near or far, even probables, don't count on a life list. With our eyes, however, we're sharp enough.

There are supposed to be some six hundred and fifty species of birds common in North America but it's only the ones that hang around our house that we get to see very often. In winter we feed the birds and we get some satisfaction from that. Along with many other lists, we keep what is called a property list and we keep it on a yearly basis. There are scores of bluebirds where five years ago there were none; not rare and fabulous birds but pleasing nonetheless. It ought to be a sign of something—our longevity as a married couple, perhaps. What I like best are the hawks riding the thermals high above the large field in front of our house in the country. It's a roundish field, sloping, cut just once a year to keep it clean, ringed on its edges by a rim of trees either green, red or overwintering. In one corner a small pond like a blue hole dropped from the sky sits where I like to see it. The hawks soar in circles above the circular field, flashing red at the tail, soaring and circling and flashing and my head spins with them and with goofy possibilities, looping the loop, until the hawks dive or disappear and jolt me down again.

When you watch birds there are many field marks you learn to look for. Size, silhouette, coloration, flight and perching patterns, habits when flocking or alone and of course those songs and calls I can't handle. Sometimes you need three or four field marks for a positive identification, sometimes one will do. You get better and better when you watch birds regularly. Even your eyes develop tricks they couldn't do before. I've noticed lately that things and people jump out at me, overlit and too well defined, from any scene I happen to be staring at. That's the way you see when you look through a decent pair of wide-angle glasses with coated lenses and, say, 8 × 35 magnification. The trouble with seeing this way is that you tend to anticipate, and often the thing you see is not the one you should be looking at.

Naturally, I've thought about being a bird but it doesn't appeal, not even to have the gift of flight. The incessant scramble for food and position and safety from raptors, all that display and defense behavior, seems to me more frantic than effective. And as for being a female bird, forget it! There's nothing lower. It's probably apoc-

ryphal but they say that birds aren't very intelligent, as
the class Aves, because they could always just fly away
from problems. They didn't have to stick around and
evolve to survive. Weather too cold? Fly away. Food running out? Bye-bye baby. But they are sensational navi-
gators, I have to admit. I wouldn't mind having an an-
cestral compass direction that worked, a homing ability
I could call my own. In any case, I'd rather watch.

Charles and Angela Shelley, no relation to old Percy
Bysshe, lived in a wide double townhouse just up the
street from Frank E. Campbell's. At Campbell's a steady
and remunerative procession of clients is wheeled in and
out, day and night, hearses often blocking the narrow
street and jamming traffic until the funeral is over and
the corpse sped to greener ground. We went frequently to
parties at the Shelleys' and we'd sometimes have to sidle
by a coffin to get to their door. It wasn't always a great
way to start the evening. Chas and Angela hadn't figured
all the angles when they bought the house. Or perhaps
the daily *memento mori* tickled Chas's funnybone. Cath-
olics are queer about these things.

I think I've known Chas forever, or at least from a
forever that matters to me. I met him early in my first
year at college when, during an intermission at Symphony Hall, he asked me for a light. I was alone that
night and we soon got to talking. Chas was a music freak
and I really liked his brogue. Irish maids at home apart,
I hadn't heard much of that sort of speech before, and
not ever from an educated mouth. There wasn't much
else to like about Chas in a physical way. Short and
plump, with a face as red as his hair, eyes glassed in, he
was hardly attractive. To make things worse, he sweated
profusely. I think it was because he had just, as he told
me, arrived at Harvard. Obviously his suits were all
wrong for the indoor climate we manufacture in this
country, pre- and post-fuel crisis. It wasn't until weeks
later that I understood that Chas wouldn't dream of buy-

ing a suit off the peg and was waiting for a delivery from his tailor in London.

With Chas and me there was never any question of a relationship except what we liked to think of as a truly Platonic one, a buddy system, if you will. Chas had already taken a degree in a prettier Cambridge than the one in which he now found himself. His field was Elizabethan English literature. I could relate to that all right. For a change of pace, he had come to Harvard to take a Master's under the tutelage of Harry Levin. Chas lived off-campus in an apartment on Channing Street not far from the Brattle Theater, where we spent many of our hours together, either upstairs at the movies or down in the bar in the basement. For the two years that our respective stays in the Boston vicinity overlapped, I guess I saw more of Chas than I saw of any one other male person. He taught me more and better than what I was learning out in the suburbs there. I couldn't believe how fine words and phrases flowed out of that little man's mouth, effortlessly, acutely. Chas was for me a well-fleshed-out Joyce: scabrous, mordant, incredibly witty and with more than a touch of the poet in him. Much easier to read than *Ulysses*, too. I wasn't the only girl who hung around with Chas. There were others, many of whom came for something other than a verbal handout. Chas may have been short and red but he was very rich, generous rich. Chas's offerings to the second sex ran to furs and cars and Caribbean weekends; not your usual collegiate philanthropy.

The only son of an only son, his father dead and his mother immured in a labyrinthine manse through which even Chas could not thread his way, Chas came from County Mayo, where I believe his family had a hold on much of the arable land. Mr. Shelley, a self-made man to whom money had accrued as honey sticks to a knife, had chosen to establish himself in the Irish countryside. It must have been a lyric antidote to the Dublin tenements that constituted his boyhood landscape. Chas told me

that his father had been a very shady character, not just
in his business dealings but paternally, the very ghost of
a father. Where the money came from was as much of a
mystery as where the affection had fled to. Chas had one
sister, older by three years, who had married a neighbor-
ing squire and was devoted to the care of her many
horses. Chas's mother, a simple woman, deeply religious, lived with a small battalion of servants in that
large house high above Clew Bay facing west over the
sea, mooning dottily of a girlhood in the friendlier streets
of Dublin. She had, I was told, a little problem with the
sauce that was scarcely alleviated by regular confession
to the local priest. Chas was groomed from the start as a
gentleman-scholar whose achievements might one day
whitewash his father's messy success. Of course Chas
had the temperament for such an upbringing, rather
liked it in fact, all the verbose preening and pecking of it.

Chas spent three years at Trinity College, Cambridge,
in a fug of dubious distinction and even more questionable sobriety. Those days were for him, he said, an atten-
uated version of Max Beerbohm's in that "other" place.
For an Elizabethan specialist Chas had some very Ed-
wardian notions, his thoughts running as they did to the
high life. I suppose that growing up with mostly tutors to
talk to hadn't prepared Chas for much but social vulner-
ability. He said he just couldn't get enough of good company, once out of that lonely Irish house, and that perhaps the best way to get it and keep it was to foot the bills
for it. Chas developed what was to remain a lifelong
habit of overdone hospitality to compensate for what, at
Trinity, was not really an exceptional mind. In an hon-
orable tradition, he barely scraped through his exams. It
wasn't until he got to Harvard that Chas began to realize
that he had a very unusual commodity sitting somewhere between his ears. Genuine British eccentrics were
not exactly a dime a dozen in Harvard Yard, especially
not ones with a gift of gab and an allowance that ran to
something slightly less than the Defense budget for all of

Great Britain. By the time Chas left Harvard, degreeless, he knew he would never live in Ireland again. Nor in England, where he hadn't really gone over very well. He was, he said, quite addicted to America. I was, I said, going to miss him sorely.

Chas went to New York and started his positioning play. All of this I heard later because I was still finishing out my sentence up north and, what with one thing and another, I didn't catch up with Chas until I came back to New York after six years as a very married lady. Chas had married too; I'll get to that. Chas bought into a small publishing house that was the hobby of an elderly gentleman, Yale '14, whose backlist consisted of improbably elegant items. Within six months the old gent was dead of what may have been astonishment. Chas chose to bring into the literary world a series of publications that exemplified, in the worst way, poetry as it is written by undergraduates with a taste for the macabre and even nastier ideas about punctuation. Written, in fact, by many of Chas's new friends, to whom no other commercial outlet could possibly be available. One book I saw, in London, with Chas's imprint on it was by a man known all over Harvard as a Jewish Dylan Thomas, more for the curls on his fat head than for any comparable verbal abilities. It took three years for Chas to run the publishing house into the ground. No bookseller would take his titles any more and he wound up pulping most of his production. But Chas got quite a lot of mileage out of his loss. His lavish book parties, his patronage of the literati, his brogue and charm that were as thick as they had ever been, the apparently inexhaustible funds that he dispersed gladly, making him the easiest touch in New York, had all earned for Chas an indisputable territory and attracted the woman with whom he was to mate.

Angela, Angelus, Angelum: I'm probably not declining it right, as it's a long time since I did Latin. What remains, actually, of the more classic elements of my education is that I choose to use a toothpaste called Vade-mecum. Every morning, every evening, I squeeze a narrow pink stripe of high school on my toothbrush and decide, yes, to take it along into another day, *vade mecum.* Angela, another classic, was also inaccessible to me. Sacred Heart had done it again. Poised, beautifully modulated in voice and manner, sharp-witted but not sharp-tongued, pale and cool: what is it they feed those girls for lunch all those years? Angela came from a lesser suburb of Detroit, not quite Grosse Pointe. She told me that she spent four years at Mt. Holyoke losing her faith by way of majoring in philosophy and Amherst. She came to New York and lived for almost a year at the Barbizon Hotel for Women, working at odd jobs during the day for a temporary secretarial bureau that sent her wherever her skills and services were needed. Chas's office manager called the bureau when an illegible handwritten manuscript that was two months overdue came in on the very day his typist quit. Angela worked for Chas for a week, and although he wasn't in the office much he stopped by more than was his custom when he saw what was sitting at a desk in his domain. Beautiful Angela, clever Angela, to see so quickly that the time was right and not to mind the shape of things. They were married shortly.

The bald eagle has an interesting mating maneuver, one attested to by naturalists who have observed it. I've seen plenty of eagles out west and in Maine, but I've never had the luck to catch this amazing number. Wheeling, zooming, screeching, testing, perfecting their timing, the two birds fly up thousands of feet into the air and at the highest point in their flight lock talons and go into a free-fall dive, somersaulting, doing seventy, eighty miles an hour, diving until they unlock claws and break apart just a few feet above the ground so as not to smash into it. Sometime during that dive they've made it together. Very sexy, I think. Bald eagles are monogamous and they pair for the life of either bird.

Angela and I did not have much to say to each other. I was living in New York again, working, we both had three children, hers slightly older than mine and all girls, but that hardly guaranteed good conversation. As Chas's former buddy, I and my husband were on the Shelleys' B list for a while, although I suspect that Angela preferred guests whose addresses could be verified in the Social Register or at the very least in a Who's Who. How she put up with some of Chas's yeastier poets and scholars is beyond me. Angela was very active in certain medical and Catholic charities. She often modeled at the fashion luncheons that those two groups go in for in a fun but not very profitable way. As I hadn't known Angela before, I had to suppose that what I saw was what she was, a person for whom the small details of life played a big part. Angela paid a great deal of attention to things like properly pedigreed furniture and elaborate food and servants and flowers. Their apartment was a bower of exotic blooms, a hothouse that was as beautiful as it seemed artificial. Once, at a dinner party late in September, a guest was so overcome by the centerpiece that he was rushed to the Lenox Hill emergency room for Adrenalin shots to mitigate his convulsive sneezes. The flowers that night were nifty arrangements of goldenrod, ragweed and other seasonal poisons. Angela's girls were big contributors to the hothouse effect. One more delicate and finer than the next, I always saw them wearing the smocked Liberty floral print dresses that Fortnum's is famous for. During cocktails, early in the evening, they would come to make their curtsies, led into the library by Nanny Thompson, who starched them and their dresses so well. It was all very darling.

I found Chas changed, somewhat deodorized. In place of the boisterous humor he used to be so free with, a kind of rigor charmis had set in, a lockjaw smile that stretched the mouth but didn't rumple it, as if Nanny Thompson had done a job on him too. And Chas didn't seem altogether comfortable in Angela's Georgian-silver-toast-rack-as-letter-holder scheme of interior decoration. It may have been too restrained, restraining, for a man of so many excesses. But Chas was immensely proud of Angela and he had a real fix on those children, rare creatures he had not imagined could come out of his stubby loins. Indulgent, expansive, Chas coddled the females in his life as perfections he wasn't quite worthy of. After the publishing house had failed, Chas started a magazine, a trendy rag that was supposed to appear quarterly but didn't. I think Chas was aiming for something like an academic *Tatler*. Chas wrote long prefatory remarks to each issue, commenting on the contents and on matters of interest in general. Reading his prefaces, about all that was really digestible in that magazine, I was glad to see that Chas's inventive mind had not gone the way of his mouth. Chas was no longer the grand talker that he had been. For one thing, he was drinking heavily and by nine in the evening was usually to be found in a state of merry inarticulation.

It was at about this time that Chas's mother died in Ireland. He and Angela flew over for the funeral and to make appropriate noises with his lawyers there. Chas had been left the house, among other things, and he promptly gave it away to his sister, who wanted it. He also instructed his lawyers to dispose of all his properties, real and paper ones. He wanted, he said, to be in a position of utter liquidity in America. The Shelleys brought back to New York with them a number of lesser paintings by great English painters, Stubbs, Reynolds, Romney and so on. The elder Mr. Shelley had clearly been the victim of some very unscrupulous dealings. Chas and Angela also brought back a manservant, Coole, Coolie, Chas called him, whom even I had heard about years before. Coolie had been head groom when Chas was a boy and had eventually been promoted to an indoor post and up as far as butler. Coolie had nursed Chas's mother through her extended and difficult death. Chas used to tell me that Coolie taught him everything he knew of a nonscholastic nature: how to smoke, what to drink when, how to shoot, to drive and how to avoid a dose. The essential lessons of boyhood that aren't always forthcoming from fathers whose shadows obscure their intentions. Coolie, in his late sixties, tall and spare, a bodily reversed Sancho Panza to Chas's chubby Quixote, was to function in the Shelley household as confidant, chauffeur, exchequer and general picker-upper of the pieces Chas tended to scatter around himself in an effort to make absolutely everybody happy.

There's a strange bird in Africa, one kind of hornbill, that practices what is called walling. What the male does is dig up dirt, which he mixes with spittle and dung; it's the female who does the heavy work, the plastering, walling herself into a nest in a hollow tree. For three or four months at a time she lives in darkness, isolation, with only a tiny hole piercing the wall for her beak to stick out of so that the male can feed her. In that bricked-up retreat she lays, broods, hatches and cares for her young, molting all the time, becoming flightless. One fine day she bursts out from behind that wall, her chicks and her feathers half-grown and the hell with it.

With all that money close to hand, the Shelleys started showing signs of a migratory restlessness. Like certain waterfowl, they seemed to be afflicted with what looks to experienced observers like nonsense orientation, a veering here and there, shifting, turning, searching for a track to travel on. In April the Shelleys bought a house in Southampton, on Meadow Lane, not far from the converted carriage house they had been renting for the past several summers. Angela described the house to me as "very Newport." I hoped what she had in mind was fidelity to the shingle style but, as I never saw the house, I can't be sure. The following February Chas and Angela acquired another property, a house on Hobe Sound about which I heard little because Angela preferred to talk about the 75-foot cruiser that had come with the house.

The yacht, which they renamed *Heaven!*, a much-used Shelley expression of approval, had a permanent crew of four who would sail it up to Southampton in the summers and back down to Florida every winter. A year later Chas bought the house near Campbell's. With homes as ubiquitous as Dr. Gucci's loafers, Angela turned now to the task of making them as comfortable as those gorgeous shoes. A well-known decorator was retained to help Angela achieve the effects she so desired.

Chas's magazine appeared seven times in almost five years and then it died the death it deserved, mourned by no one but Coolie, who hadn't read it. When you totted up just Chas's residential and business expenditures over the same period, you could see what was making Coolie nervous. Done forever with publishing in any form, Chas started in the brokerage business after a long vacation with Angela in southern France. Chas worked out of a small house that was glad to give him desk space in return for the increase in volume cleared through their firm. Every day Coolie drove Chas downtown and back up again. It was the most regular employment that Chas had ever attempted. As I understood it from friends on the Street, Chas's transactions consisted primarily of buying and selling for his own account, and he took the kind of fliers that could only be computed as sumptuary suicide. Rather than launder what he surely thought of as his father's dirty money, Chas was simply letting it run down a voracious drainpipe whose outlet soiled several different seas. Angela, throughout, seemed unchanged, maybe a bit more brittle than she had been but still determined to make her way in a world that was always perfectible. Either Angela didn't notice that Chas's inheritance was sloshing away or else she liked the noise the water made. About Chas's drinking Angela could and did do nothing. That, basically, was Coolie's business.

Something about faith. It figures, I guess, although I'm not sure just how, or even what it was. Angela may have recouped hers somewhere along the way; we never discussed it a second time. The girls were all at Sacred Heart and Chas told me that the older one was wonderfully devout, a dreamer, longing for beatitude and all the mortifications that preadolescent girls make a specialty of. She had, Chas said, a possible vocation. As for Chas, he never lost what he called "m'faith." Curious. I would have thought, given Chas's declared interests in the fleshier facts of life, the materiality of it, that his belief might have doused itself long ago in some humid Irish boghole. Not so. Chas insisted when I asked him once that it was his religion and the design it imposed that gave any order at all to his life. I have to assume that Chas spent a lot of time sorting and grading sins into confessional schemata that would get them off his back.

In the hole with a net loss of three million dollars, Chas quit Wall Street after a year and turned full-time to the entertaining charades that he and Angela had constructed in lieu of a working life. They partied and traveled and were big collectors, amassing flocks, great chic hordes, of people and quality merchandise around themselves. I was not really on their list any more, so the rest is based on what I could see from a considerable remove and on what I heard about Chas. You didn't hear too much about Angela.

Many birds when threatened by egg- or chick-loving predators perform decoy behavior that varies, species-wise, from the simple to the highly complex. The object being, of course, to protect the young and thereby ensure the continuation of the species, a matter of little concern to the California condor, certain herons and doves, who abandon their nests altogether when disturbed. I've seen it all, except for rodent running, so this is firsthand. There are essentially two techniques: distraction displays that either mislead the predator as to the location of the nest or decoy the intruder away from it, and threat displays that are meant to startle and scare the son of a bitch away. The latter method is made up of tricks like sudden color and size changes, simulated explosions of feathers, general abusive shrieking and diving, often as a mob, and other such aggressive commotions. The distraction behavior runs to tactics like plain sneaking away from the nest, or false brooding, when a bird sits in a fake nest on stones that look like a clutch of eggs, or rodent running, when a purple sandpiper dashes madly, puffing up his tail feathers to resemble the furry behind of a tasty rodent, or self-prostration. The self-prostration techniques include imitation of juveniles, diversionary hysteria and, the most common, broken-wing behavior, when a bird appears to be helpless and available but, in the nick of time, can escape the predator, who had been lured far from the nest.

Chas went on several sorts of binges. First of all, he set out to disprove, single-handedly, that rusty saw about the rich getting richer. Within the span of the next three years Chas's liquid assets had been converted into solid liabilities. Chas owed money everywhere. He had finally gotten rid of the last of his father's gift to him. How Chas must have hated that old bugger to have mocked him so! The bills piled up but the style did not appear to be much reduced. *Heaven!* cruised and Southampton threw open its own pearly gates to almost anyone who knocked on them and the flowers continued to blossom in such adverse circumstances. The puzzling thing was that Chas seemed to have an elastic credit line, one on which he could bounce as on a trampoline, up and over and down and up again, as long as he kept his wits about him. Angela, never very athletic, began to cut back in a modest way, and Coolie must have been beside himself with the worrying.

Chas's second extravanganza was quite as wanton as his fiscal blowout, more so perhaps when you consider that he was fouling his own nest. Chas had certainly had other women all along, I knew of a few myself, but he had never actually installed an official mistress before.

In a manner that I thought went out with the latter kings
of France, Chas established his *belle horizontale* in an
apartment on Sutton Place that was, I heard, a glazier's
delight: smoky mirrors everywhere. Small dinner parties
and so forth were given once a week in that apartment,
to which invitations were as scarce as flamingos and
probably as showy. There are few things in this day and
age that are truly villainous and adultery is not one of
them. I'm sure that even Angela, walled in the dark as
she had been, insulated by cash and her Catholicism,
had learned as we all have to tolerate infidelities of a
confidential nature. It was the public aspect of Chas's
affront to her that Angela found unacceptable. Angela
countered with what was for her some fairly radical action. She scooped up the children and took them to her
parents' house in Michigan for a visit that lasted many,
many months. Coolie she left in New York, where he had
his hands full.

Chas's greatest excess, one which had shoved him
downwind all along, was the drink. Bloated, tousled, red-
der and wetter than ever, I saw him walking up Madison
Avenue one morning and when we stopped to kiss and
tell Chas had trouble breathing, speaking. Broken-wing,
all right. And more. A blithe spirit damped and brutish,
mortified by indignities of a sort his daughter wouldn't
have dreamed of, an immolation on some crazy cross he
bore and yet couldn't bear to part with. I asked after Angela and the children and Chas told me they were all
back together in the house next to Campbell's. Hobe
Sound and *Heaven!* were gone and they were trying to
sell New York and move to Southampton. Angela's ulti-
matum: a country life. The older girl, too suggestible by
far, had stayed with her grandparents in Michigan and
he missed her, he reminded me, sorely.

As far as I know, Angela still lives in Southampton,
with Coolie to care for her and the girls. Coolie must be
close to eighty by now and I'm sure he copes. Some
months after settling them on Meadow Lane, Chas van-

ished. Angela works more and plays, I hear, a bit less. She gets enough money from her parents to keep up the house and herself and the children. Many but not all of Chas's debts were paid off with money realized from the sale of the house in New York and its splendid contents. For Angela, no divorce will happen and I am told it does not matter to her. Chas hasn't been seen or heard from. Even Coolie doesn't know where or if he is.

On some islands, in trees, on lake bottoms and on hill-tops, there are bird boneyards, mass graves of grounded creatures. No one is quite sure whether the bones are brought to these places or whether a bird flies here to die. I've never come across such an ossuary but I can see it anyway, high heaps of bright bones turned wormy.

XIII

I had an old friend who showed me, recently, how division really works. One into one makes one, two into one makes a half, thirty-five into one makes difficulties, that kind of division. Even though I was never tops in arithmetic it's one of those basic operations I thought I had mastered years ago in grade school; how to handle divisors and decimals and quotients and remainders, estimating and rounding off to the nearest whole and so on. I hadn't but I have now. Mastered it. Almost.

I first met Hélène Delveaux at Maison de la Harpe pour Jeunes Filles, an establishment in which we both served time and perhaps some other, greater good. La Harpe is situated on the slope below the main street that runs through the formerly quaint and currently spotless village of Villars in the French-speaking part of Switzerland. Walking along this main street, just above la Harpe, you can look over a railing and down onto the blotchy red of the tennis court. In the afternoons there will be girls on the court. Various flags hang from poles on the porch that runs across the long side of the large and gabled chalet, representing the nationalities of the girls housed therein. About forty-five of us lived in this brown house for our French and our manners: acquiring, polishing, whatever. All lessons, explanations grammatical and otherwise, conversation, table talk and entertainments were conducted in French. Roommates never came from the same country and so were presumed by Madame to communicate only in French. Even our letters home, supervised, had to be written in French. The girls were, and I suppose still are, English, Italian, German, Iranian and South American. There were very few French girls and even fewer Americans in the several summers I spent at la Harpe. Anyone who came to la Harpe not knowing any French at all could not and never did last more than a week. Emergency departures for curious medical reasons were frequent occurrences.

In the mornings we had lessons. We filled book after little blue book with words and phrases that would never cross our lips in the course of any ordinary conversation. During those years I had, in New York, a French tutor of similarly archaic persuasions, so I was not wholly out of my depth at la Harpe. After lessons came lunch and a rest, followed by sports and excursions. The excursions consisted of walks in the alpine fields above the village or a promenade to the post office. The sports were tennis on our own court or swimming in the ice-cold pool at the Palace Hotel. The hotel overlooks the town like a vast and indulgent uncle, each window winking, every balcony curved in a little smile, but the management's benevolence did not extend to heating the water in the pool and none of us could stand it very long. Chaperones for these outings almost outnumbered their charges and we walked in two straight lines, like Madeline. After dinner we sat in the living room and sang or listened to stories or, worse, recited dramatic poetry of the sort that only the French can manufacture. You can tell that I am speaking of the days before mass addiction to television, when finishing was still a term that applied to girls as it did to furniture. Once a week the older girls would go to Beausoleil, a similar school for boys, farther down the same slope. When the boys came to la Harpe we could hear music coming from the old gramophone in the dining room. There were thick red curtains on the glass doors of the dining room, so we couldn't see if anyone was actually dancing. Lights out at nine-thirty. That's when our day began. We dropped out of French and into action. Almost everyone spoke some sort of English and that was the principal language in which our black-marketeering was conducted. The major commodities were food, bras, comic books and flashlight batteries. Most of the commercial activity was carried out by the middle-aged girls, of whom I was one. The older girls were too busy debating whether or not to sneak out, or were in fact sneaking out, to keep the rendezvous they had made with boys from Beausoleil. The top floor bathroom was used as an escape hatch. We were sworn to secrecy, in return for which we demanded a steady supply of tradeable goods. In this fashion romance, extortion and business flourished.

The summer that I was thirteen I cornered the market in bananas at la Harpe. It was the same summer I had a French roommate, Hélène, whom I did not like one bit. Hélène was docile and too beautiful by far to share a room with someone who wasn't. Her looks I ignored as best I could and her meekness turned out to be an asset to me. Hélène said she hated the sweet stench coming from the pounds of bananas I had stored in the back of the single closet in our room. She claimed the smell was like the one that issues from certain butcher shops whose item of trade is indicated by the model of a horse's head, often golden, hung over their doorways. Hélène spoke like that, very precious, I thought, very Parisian. I couldn't agree about the smell because horse meat, along with beauty and docility, was not in my personal vocabulary. Hélène threatened several times a day to tell Madame about the bananas but I knew she didn't have the nerve to interfere with my booming business and I was right. We spent a month despising each other. I never wrote to Hélène after the summer nor she to me although out of politeness, more hers than mine, we had exchanged addresses. Fifteen years later Hélène came back into my life and changed it. It happened in the following way. One more thing. You should know that my husband was a Beausoleil boy and he says he remembers those dim and graceless soirées at la Harpe. Of course he was there well before my time but, still, it pleases me.

There's a particular stretch of Fifth Avenue that is dotted with a series of oval playgrounds that were, in the sixties when I used them, as tripartite as Gaul under Caesar. Mothers, white nurses and black housekeepers were the three components of the sharp and tyrannical partition that made even the children uneasy. Each faction appropriated precisely the same benches every day, or at least they did so in the mornings, which is when I took my children out. If some innocent sat down in the wrong camp, she was quickly made aware of her error by a combination of looks and mutters that was so chilling it generally sent her straight home. Out of sheer and quite tolerable perversity, I sat alone on the no-man's-bench between the black and white help. Sitting with the mothers, who always took the sunny side, was hot and noisy and the conversation was too pediatric and scholastic to suit me. On the help's side the children seldom whined and I could concentrate on my reading. I spoke French to my children partly to avoid being spoken to and partly, I suspect, in an effort to please my French-born husband with what he would call *gentille* behavior. (*"Gentille maman. Regarde comme elle parle bien le français, ta gentille maman."* The French have a great flair for reducing even complex relationships to the level of yum-yum talk.) One day my son took a serious bite out of the hand of a dwarf terrorist in the sandbox. I had to scold him: every eye was on me. I let him have it in French and managed to insinuate my not-total disapproval of his act. A tiny blonde woman rose from a bench and came to stare at me. Hélène. And so it began.

We caught up quickly in the months that followed. The bananas were remembered and forgotten. I had been to college, spent a year in London, and had married a doctor whose training took us to Boston for a few years before he started a practice in New York. I was about to go to work in the afternoons at a job that I figured would keep me out of Bendel's and mischief and, if nothing else, would provide me with a ready and acceptable answer to dinner partners who made it their business to inquire into mine. Hélène had studied at the Sorbonne for five years and had taken two degrees in medieval history. She had married an American living in France—an investment banker doing a *stage* in his firm's Paris office —Peter Thornton, whom she called Pierre. Hélène had become a remarkably ornamental woman. She looked, with her fugitive coloring, like one of the Japanese porcelains that Pierre collected with an interest that bordered on obsession. Hélène was splendidly and expensively dressed, her glaze clear and fine. I, in contrast, had fulfilled some earlier Mediterranean promises and was somewhat more erratic about putting myself together.

Hélène and Pierre had just recently moved their two young boys and their old wines to New York. They lived a few blocks away from us in a large duplex apartment that was, apart from tall glass vitrines filled with those impeccable porcelains, surprisingly empty. On rainy mornings I would sometimes take my children to ride their tricycles in one of Hélène's spare rooms while we had coffee in the library. We both loved food, traveling, mothering, tennis and Simenon, so we had a lot to talk about when we sat together at her house or in the playground. I was as glad for Hélène's company as I think she was for mine. My place on that bench in the DMZ was by then losing whatever charm I had forced upon it. And I knew very few women besides Hélène, in our neighborhood, who took their children to the park in the mornings. Everyone I liked was back in school or working full-time or was out volunteering as if charity didn't begin where they left off. Staying at home and minding the store had begun to look like positively reactionary behavior and no one wants to be a back number.

Pierre and my husband got on very well, both devoutly Francophile, both soccer and World War II nuts, both intelligent listeners. Our friendship had a certain mutuality from all angles. Pierre was at the top of one heap that counted, in those days. The art world then was a way of life and I don't mean for painters and sculptors. If you had money, any money at all, you bought objects as visas to a country that was pleasantly small and accessible. Out in California, down in Mississippi, people were plunging into the heavy floodwaters of rights and wrongs. In New York they weren't having much of that because they were too busy in a puddle of fun, collecting emblems of value like Boy Scouts going after merit badges, overzealously and a bit indiscriminately. I must admit right now that my husband and I were collecting art in a minor way and for a few of those same reasons. So I was Hélène's friend and we all had some fun together but I couldn't be a close friend to Hélène. There was a softness I saw beyond the blue of her eyes that didn't tempt me at all and, not that I want now to excuse myself, it is true that I didn't have much time for Hélène, not any more. In what seemed like a brief but profuse period, my life had expanded as helium does, puffing up to fill and stretch a skin to the bursting point.

Speaking inventorially, I was possessed of and by one husband, three children in three schools, two residences, a job, one cranky housekeeper, a colitic rabbit, three gerbils in three cages and a volatile and demanding circle of family, friends and cherishable artifacts around me. I was cook, collector, eldest daughter, class mother and big sister, part-time careerist and indefatigable shopper, reader and telephonic consumer. Not to mention vacations (plenty), entertainment (excessive), lunches (chronic) and (a few) unmentionables. My engagement book looked like the inside of a rush-hour subway train, crowded and unyielding. I wasn't quite going in the proverbial forty directions but I was headed in thirty-five at the very least and I have to say I didn't really mind it. So if I saw less and less of Hélène over the next couple of years it wasn't for reasons of disaffection but because of the time factor, which is a New York and insufficient reason. Such a pop-top world we live in, where convenience is the cutting edge. When I spoke to Hélène on the telephone, twice a week usually, it took long minutes for our conversations to get going. We made dates and she very often broke them, confirming my belief that she was even busier than I was. One date she didn't break was an invitation one weekend in May to our house in the country, with the children, naturally.

Now, I fix on the accident as a junction more essential than la Harpe or any playground. Two paths really crossed here. There's a marker in the form of a scar I see every day on my daughter's face and there are marks I can not see. Images blurred as the new green of May leaves, steam rising from a heated pool into the air, the children's voices, legs pumping and feet skidding, a glass door shatters against a face, slicing skin and bone. I did not see but heard this. A thin minute of silence before the blood flows. My husband and I went to the hospital. Hélène and Pierre closed up the house and took all the other children back to New York. Hélène's words to me seven hours later were *"ma faute"* and she was shaking when I came to fetch my children from her apartment. Pierre was upstairs, telephoning. The next morning Hélène arrived at nine, still shaking, and sat all day with my daughter, who in her long bathrobe looked like a miniature Claude Rains with part of the bandaging on his invisible head unwrapped. I called Pierre, who said something about tranquilizers that I didn't quite catch. Hélène spoke so quietly. It was her children who had wanted to swim, she said, on a gray day, rushing the season, even before the caretaker had thought to put in the screens, everyone running and slamming doors to get into the water faster. I made random sounds, trying to talk about the blamelessness of accidents. Hélène insisted. For reasons of my own, I let her.

Wounds close, proud flesh forms to heal our scars and we go on, vulnerable but forward, adjustable. In a room in that apartment not far from where we live was a chair in which Hélène sat and went over and over and over but not on. It wasn't just glass that shattered and a month later Hélène went away for the first time.

When Hélène came back from Silver Hill, well into the winter of the following year, I could see a change in her. While she had in some way been energized she had in some other way been decentralized. Hélène was like French toast, in French called *pain perdu,* lost bread, a runny whitemelt barely contained by its brittle and sugary crusts. Hélène's aristocracy, her fine finish that I had always admired even when it upset me at la Harpe, had been smeared and blunted beyond the mere coming apart of a seam or two. Hélène was as irritable as she was irritating, thorny and vituperative, flurried. She smoked and argued incessantly and her arguments were punctuated with a remote and fraudulent laughter, a kind of gaping and sputtering and working of the mouth into what was finally no more than the facsimile of a smile. Hélène wore dark glasses and astonishingly bright clothes and she seemed to be having a lot of trouble in the upper respiratory region. On the few occasions we had dinner with them Hélène spoke mostly to my husband and they talked medicine. It's hard to believe that competent doctors in a respectable place like Silver Hill could have let Hélène think that she might one day get into medical school but that, it appears, is what happened.

I haven't said much about Pierre. He's smart and I find him very attractive and he's a gentle man but there's a breezy way he has with me that I can't understand. I keep thinking I should matter to him and I don't. If I hadn't sat next to Pierre on a flight to Europe last year, purely by chance, I might never have heard some things about Hélène that I had only been able to guess at. Some things about her family and her pregnancies, about her nervous past that surfaced in gestation, especially the second time around, and about the acutely protective nature of Pierre's feelings for his sons.

Hélène informed me that she slept late in the mornings and read in the afternoons. Biology and anatomy texts and so forth. It was a regular if not quite reasonable arrangement. She and Pierre seldom went out at night any more and they were away from New York for weeks at a time. My friendship with Hélène had been demoted to a biweekly call I made to her when she was in town. Hélène never called me but she called my husband at all hours of the day and night when she needed some scientific explanation. Hélène often came to his office, he told me, to watch him work. My husband is a patient man. He put Hélène into a white lab coat and passed her off as one of his nurses, sometimes. My husband attempted, as I did when I spoke to her, to dissuade Hélène from pursuing a course we doubted she could achieve with any measure of success. It was tricky because we didn't want to move her out of focus, only to move her.

You ought to know that despite the inflated inventory of my life I suffer from three major American cultural deprivations. I've never been to Southern California, I've never owned my own car (although I drive pretty well), and I've never been psychoanalyzed (it could be beneficial). California and the car don't really count in this context but the analysis might have. If I hadn't been so unsavvy, so uninfuckingformed, I might have recognized sooner the utterly turbulent distress signals that Hélène was putting out and that Pierre was putting away like ancient prisoners in an oubliette. I'm not exactly deaf and I'm not exactly dumb but I didn't get Hélène's message. Not until later. There's a kind of antelope, pronghorn I think, that heliographs danger by secreting an oily substance onto its white rump and using the sun's rays on that slick surface, mirrorlike, to warn the rest of the herd that danger is imminent. Hélène's clothes, that impossible laughter, her discourtesy, should have tipped me off about her inner order or lack of it. I guess I had my head down too long, grazing, chomping blindly, feeding my own face. It may have been that, message received, I would have been helpless anyway. But then again, maybe not. I'm sure now that I should have, could have, tried harder to help prevent Hélène from slipping and sliding through the icy funnel of confusion that was her mind then. I mean I could have interfered if nothing else. I could have called her mother or taken a loudmouthed stand against Pierre's tactic of concealment or found another, better doctor for her. I was her oldest friend in New York. We dated back. We shared a history and some scars. I owed it to her. *Ma faute* that I was ignorant and, yes, busy.

Of course it happened that Hélène went back to Silver Hill. Some still impenetrable event occurred, late one night. I suspect that Hélène slashed a part of her body or of her children's bodies. Slashing and burning is what some primitive tribes do to speed up their crop cycle. It will in turn render those fields untillable, infertile. I have studied this and I know it to be true. I have also observed at first hand how the slashing of human skin is an irreversible act, plastic surgery notwithstanding. Slashing of skin is a prominent method in the human attempt to efface itself. Pills pass through, gas vanishes into the air, but slashing sticks. The blade intrudes: a maximal gesture, the loudest voice. I did not hear it.

It took only a few months for Hélène to come home this time, although she didn't actually come home but went instead to live in a hotel. Pierre said the doctors didn't want her living with the children. And anyway, he said, she was cramming for the medical school aptitude examinations and needed to study undisturbed. If she came to visit, we were on no account to give her anything to drink but fruit juices and soft drinks. Alcohol and the drugs she was on were not compatible. That's what Pierre said and that's all he said.

I went once to the hotel but Hélène was not there. I went again and she was in her room but would not answer the telephone, so the desk clerk quite properly did not let me go up. I left messages for a week and then I stopped calling. I was working at home one afternoon when the doorbell rang at three-thirty and Hélène was there, flickering on my doorstep like a firefly trapped too long in a jar. I was not ready for death and the way she looked. Hair cropped and reddened, her eyes granulated behind the glasses, tattered and slack, Hélène came in and broke my heart in advance of what I knew would happen and perhaps soon. In a terrible and loud voice she explained that she came every afternoon to see, that is to look at from afar, her children leaving their school, which was on our block. She had asked the doorman if I was home, she said, she knew I wouldn't mind. The children, she said, looked fine.

Hélène came almost every day in the two months that followed, and sat for an hour or more reading her textbooks, taking notes. At first I called Pierre and he said please, to let her. I went to work early and made it my business to be home by three every day. Hélène rarely spoke and when she did, what we had could not be called conversation. Hélène read and I sat watching her, pretending to occupy myself with whatever busy-work I could put my hands on, bills, sewing, such nonsense. If my children wandered into the room in which I sat with Hélène, they didn't stay very long. They must have sensed the stink that lay beneath the smell of our cigarettes, a rank and final odor that they didn't dare to ask about. When I went into the kitchen to start dinner Hélène would read in there, perched at a counter like a pile of old clothes waiting for the thrift-shop pickup. Hélène wouldn't stay for dinner when I asked her and she always left before my husband came home because she didn't want, she said, to see him, not like this.

I said before that Hélène changed my life. It was on those difficult afternoons that a change was starting to take place. What I mean is that Hélène changed what will be my death. The life part I have to do myself.

I've read somewhere that Sainte-Beuve, dying, drew pictures of his intestinal cancer so that visitors to his sickroom would have an instructive souvenir to take home with them. I had Hélène to map it out for me. Her diagram was suddenly so clear and real. You don't have to have a disease to know how it can kill, to make such equations. Hélène made me see that death is division, long or short. I saw it, I finally saw it. It's being divisible that diminishes the life we have, the chance we have, the death we make. Cleft, disjunct and fractional, we lose the whole. Events and people pluck at us from every side and we fibrillate, shrilling and twanging a tune that isn't ours to twang. I saw that it wasn't what I wanted for myself, not such abusive music.

Except for a couple of months one year in college, I had never thought much about dying. One grandmother died when I was twelve and a favorite uncle a few years later and my sister's baby and six million others but those were not my deaths, not possibly. When Hélène splintered and eroded before my very eyes I took it as a warning, a light flashing to slow me down and make me look around, maybe to stop me. It was definitely *nel mezzo del cammin* but I figured *nel mezzo* is better than never.

I saw that going in thirty-five directions wasn't going

to get me anywhere at all and not in one piece either, so I did some things I thought might simplify the numbers. I subtracted. Subtraction is another one of those basic operations. I took away the unnecessary from my life, the fat of it, which turned out to be a great deal of it. For starters, I quit the job that was undermining me. I kicked, cold, my telephone, lunch and department-store habits. I didn't exactly get rid of my possessions but I took away caring about them. I didn't exactly dump my friends and family but I took away looking for endorsement, approval, in their eyes. I stopped letting strangers play their games on my turf, on my time. I stopped getting ready, on my mark, for a race I don't want to run in any more. I stopped regretting and I stopped resenting. I stopped depending. I stopped and I started. I started counting. One into one makes one, makes one, makes me one, makes me, makes my tune to whistle as I walk right along and along and out.

About the Author

Lucienne S. Bloch was educated in New York City and at Wellesley College. In 1959 she was awarded the Joyce Glueck Poetry Prize by the New England Poetry Society; she has also received the Academy of American Poets Award.

She lives in New York City with her husband and three children, and is at work on a second novel.